PENGUIN BOOKS

REVENGE OF THE MOONCAKE VIXEN

Marilyn Chin was born in Hong Kong in 1955 and spent the first few years of her life being called Mei Ling. It was only when she moved to the United States soon after with her family that her father insisted that the change in location be reflected in a change of name for Mei Ling – to Marilyn, after Marilyn Monroe.

Marilyn Chin has won numerous awards for her poetry, including four Pushcart Prizes. Her books of poetry include *The Phoenix Gone, the Terrace Empty*, *Dwarf Bamboo* and *Rhapsody in Plain Yellow*. *Revenge of the Mooncake Vixen* is her first novel.

REVENGE OF THE MOONCAKE VIXEN

A MANIFESTO IN 41 TALES

Marilyn Chin

PENGUIN BOOKS

PENGUIN BOOKS

Published by the Penguin Group

Penguin Books Ltd, 80 Strand, London WC2R ORL, England

Penguin Group (USA) Inc., 375 Hudson Street, New York, New York 10014, USA

Penguin Group (Canada), 90 Eglinton Avenue East, Suite 700, Toronto, Ontario, Canada M4P 2Y3
(a division of Pearson Penguin Canada Inc.)

Penguin Ireland, 25 St Stephen's Green, Dublin 2, Ireland (a division of Penguin Books Ltd)

Penguin Group (Australia), 250 Camberwell Road,
Camberwell, Victoria 3124, Australia (a division of Pearson Australia Group Pty Ltd)

Penguin Books India Pvt Ltd, 11 Community Centre, Panchsheel Park,
New Delhi – 110 017, India

Penguin Group (NZ), 67 Apollo Drive, Rosedale, Auckland 0632, New Zealand
(a division of Pearson New Zealand Ltd)

Penguin Books (South Africa) (Pty) Ltd, 24 Sturdee Avenue, Rosebank, Johannesburg 2196, South Africa

Penguin Books Ltd, Registered Offices: 80 Strand, London WC2R ORL, England

www.penguin.com

First published in the USA by W. W. Norton & Company, Inc. 2009
First published in Great Britain by Hamish Hamilton 2010
Published in Penguin Books 2011

1

Printed in England by Clays Ltd, St Ives plc

ISBN: 978–0–141–04352–4

www.greenpenguin.co.uk

MIX
Paper from
responsible sources
FSC™ C018179

Penguin Books is committed to a sustainable
future for our business, our readers and our
planet. This book is made from paper certified
by the Forest Stewardship Council.

For My Sisters

Annoyed by a pesky girl, who is dancing around in circles, making donkey ears and sassy rhymes, the young monk loses his temper and pelts her with dung. The Master scolds the monk by saying, "Don't you recognize her? She is the same little girl you pelted in a previous state of existence. And the same girl you pelted in a previous existence before that . . ." Then the Master bestows upon his pupil a continuous battery of lessons, hoping to hasten his path toward enlightenment.

Contents

4. AFTER ENLIGHTENMENT, THERE IS YAM GRUEL
   (THIRTEEN BUDDHIST TALES)

5. BEASTS OF BURDEN (SEVEN FABLES)

6. TEN VIEWS OF THE FLYING MATRIARCH

1

Mooncakes
and Matriarchs

Moon

A CHINESE AMERICAN REVENGE TALE

Moon was a little fat Chinese girl. She had a big, yellow face befitting her name. She was sad and lonely as were all little fat Chinese girls in 1999, and she had a strange, insatiable desire for a pair of trashy blond twins named Smith (no accounting for taste, of course). Every night she would wander on the beach in search of them, hoping to espy them taking a joyride around Pacific Beach in their rebuilt sky-blue convertible Impala: their long blond hair swept backward like horses' manes, their faces obscenely sunburnt, resembling ripe halves of peaches.

One chilly September evening the boys stopped to make a campfire on the beach; and Moon, feeling quite full and confident that day, descended upon them, waddling so fat, so round and shiny with sea spray. She offered them chocolate Macadamia nut clusters and began to sing, strumming a tiny lute-like instrument her grandmother sent her from China. She began singing, in an ancient falsetto, a baleful song about exiled geese winging across the horizon, about the waxing and waning of stormy seas, about children lost into the unknown depths of the new kingdom.

The boys were born and raised in "the valley" and were very unsophisticated. They were also functional illiterates and were held back twice in the fifth grade—and there was no way that they could have understood the complexities of her song. They huddled in that sporting male way and whispered surreptitiously, speaking in very short sentences between grunts or long, run-on sentences with ambiguous antecedents, so that Moon was not quite sure whether she was the subject of their discussion. Finally, the boys offered to give fat Moon a ride in the stainless-steel canoe they got for Christmas. (We know, of course, that they were up to trouble; you don't think their hospitality was sincere, do you?)

Moon graciously accepted their invitation. Actually, she was elated, given the bad state of her social life; she hadn't had a date for centuries. So the two boys paddled, one fore, one aft, with fat Moon in the middle. Moon was so happy that she started strumming her lute and singing the song of Hiawatha. (Don't ask me why; this was what she felt like singing.) Suddenly, the boys started rocking the boat forcefully—forward and backward— making wild horsy sounds until the boat flipped over, fat Moon, lute, and all.

The boys laughed and taunted Moon to reappear from the rough water. When she didn't surface after a few minutes, it suddenly occurred to them that she was drowning; they watched in bemusement while the last of her yellow forehead bled into the waves. Finally, they dove in and dragged her heavy body back into the boat, which was quite a feat for she was twice as heavy wet than dry—and she was now tangled in sea flora.

When they finally docked, Moon discovered that the boys saved her only to humiliate her. It appeared that they wanted a reward for saving her life—a blood-debt, if you will. In this material world—where goods are bartered for goods—actions, however heroic or well intentioned in appearance, are never clearly separated from services rendered. And in the American ledger, all services must be paid for in the end, and all contracts must be signed at closing, bearing each participant's legal signature. Thus, the boys ripped off Moon's dress and took turns pissing all over her round face and belly, saying, "So, it's true, it's true that your cunts are really slanted. Slant-eyed cunt! Did you really think that we had any interest in you?"

After the boys finished their vile act, they left Moon on the wharf without a stitch on, glowing with yellow piss. And she cried, wailed all the way home on her bicycle. Imagine a little fat Chinese girl, naked, pedaling, wailing.

When Moon got home, her mother called her a slut. Her father went on and on about the Sino-Japanese war and about the starving girlchildren in Guangdong—and look, what are you doing with your youth and new prosperity, wailing, carrying on, just because some trashy white boys rejected you? Have you no shame? Your cousin the sun matriculated Harvard, your brothers the stars all became engineers . . . where are the I. M. Peis and Yo Yo Mas of your generation? They sent her to bed without supper that night as a reminder that self-sacrifice is the most profound virtue of the Chinese people.

Up in her room, Moon brooded and swore on a stack of bibles that she would seek revenge for this terrible incident—and that if she were to die today, she would come back to earth as an angry ghost to haunt those motherfuckers. With this in mind, Moon swallowed a whole bottle of sleeping pills, only to cough them back up ten minutes later. Obviously, they didn't kill her. However, those ten minutes of retching must have prevented oxygen from entering her brain and left her deranged for at least a month after this episode. (Hey, I'm no doctor, just a storyteller, take my diagnosis with caution, please.) Overnight, she became a homicidal maniac. A foul plague would shroud all of southern California, one that, curiously, infected only blond men. (Both natural and peroxided types, those slightly hennaed would be spared.)

For thirty days and thirty nights Moon scoured the seaside, howling, windswept—in search of blond victims. They would drown on their surfboards, or collapse while polishing their cars. They would suffocate in their sleep next to their wives and lovers. Some died leaving a long trail of excrement because whatever pursued them was so terrible that it literally scared the shit out of them. And not since Herod had we seen such a devastating assault on male children.

On the thirty-first night, the horror subsided. Moon finally found the Smith boys cruising in their sky-blue convertible Impala. They were driving south on the scenic coast route between San Clemente and Del Mar when she plunged down on them, her light was so powerful and bright that the boys were momentarily blinded and swerved into a canyon. Their car turned over twelve times. They were decapitated—the coroner said, so cleanly as if a surgeon had done the job with a laser.

Moon grew up, lost weight and became a famous singer, which proves that there is no justice in the universe, or that indeed, there is justice. Your interpretation of this denouement mostly depends on your race, creed, hair color, social and economic class and political proclivities—and whether or not you are a feminist revisionist and have a habit of cheering for the underdog. What is the moral of the story? Well, it's a tale of revenge, obviously written from a Chinese American girl's perspective. My intentions are to veer you away from teasing and humiliating little chubby

Chinese girls like myself. And that one wanton act of humiliation you perpetuated on the fore or aft of that boat on my arrival may be one humiliating act too many. For although we are friendly neighbors, you don't really know me. You don't know the depth of my humiliation. And you don't know what I can do. You don't know what is beneath my doing.

Round Eyes

I woke up one morning and my slanted eyes had turned round, which was nothing to be alarmed about. It happened to my rich cousin Sunny, whose mother thought that she was too ugly to capture a rich Chinese American prince; she was gagged, sedated and abducted—then zoomed to Japan in a private airplane to a famous round-eye plastic surgeon. Well— Sunny woke up with huge, round "Madonna" eyes. They fixed her flat nose into a perky "Little Orphan Annie" one, and while she was still deep under, they gave her new mammoth "Pamela Anderson" breasts for half price.

So when I woke up with round eyes, I was not particularly surprised. But then, I thought, hey, wait a minute, my family's not rich. We don't have any money to be vain. We're immigrants who toiled in sweatshop after sweatshop. We're the poor relations that everybody spat on. Sunny's family gave us hand-me-downs and scraps that their Cairn Terriers didn't want. In the fifties, they bought my father's papers, shipped him here, and he worked as a slave cook for them in their chain of chop-suey joints for most of his life.

Of course, we were supposed to be eternally grateful. I

remember one steamy episode in which my father banged his head on their giant butcher block and said, "You want grateful! You want thanks! Here, kowtow, kowtow, ten thousand years kowtow!" He banged his head so hard that he opened a gash three inches wide, and the blood streaked down his face. Such histrionics continued until he died suddenly of a heart attack in 1989.

Sometimes I look in the mirror and expect to see my father's bloody face. But on this particularly succulent spring morning, the birds were cheeping and the dogs were barking, and in our old cracked bathroom mirror—you know, the kind that is so old that the beveled edges are yellowing—I saw the monster of my own making. This morning some Greater Mother Power had transformed me into a bona fide white girl with big round eyes. My single-creased eyelid turned double, which forced the corners that originally slanted upward to slope downward. My eyes were now as round as orbs and appeared twice as large as before. My eyeballs that were once deep brown, almost black, had suddenly lightened into a golden amber. Even my eyelashes, which were once straight and spare, became fuller and curled up against my new double lids.

I immediately felt guilty. My conscience said, "Serves you right for hating your kind, for wanting to be white. Remember that old Chinese saying, don't wish for something too hard, you might just get it—and then, what?" There were no tell-tale signs of expensive surgery—no gauze, no swelling, no pus, no nothing. When the good lord makes a miracle, she does it seamlessly. After surgery Sunny looked like Frankenstein for about two months. She was black and blue and had huge ghastly stitches. Three months later, she was a completely new person cut out from *Vogue*. She had totally reinvented herself—new clothes, new friends, new attitude. She even lost her Hong Kong accent. And there she was hanging out with the in-crowd, smoking and swearing up a storm like a rich white person, like she had a piece of the American dream in her pocket. "What did you do?" I said. "Pay for your face with your soul?"

The terrible truth is that I was desperately jealous of Sunny's new popularity. She said once, while buffing her fake nails, "We're Americans now, we have to climb that ladder of success, keep up with the Joneses . . . always one up ourselves." Well, this has become our new motto—isn't it quaint?—*"Improve ourselves Wongs."* Sunny's family started this trickle-down effect. In the eighties, the fierce Reaganite competition and struggle for status in Sunny's family infected ours like the plague. Every day, after my father's death, my mother would come home from her long day's work at the factory and scowl blankly at us. My sister and I—we were never good enough, pretty enough, smart enough. My mother was the sacrificial tree on which the next crop was supposed to flourish and bear beautiful fruit—only the present harvest was not quite ready. We were an anemic batch, or one too hard, or green and small to bring a good barter at the market. My mother would scrutinize us in her sleepy sadness and sob, then fold herself up in bed and not come out again until it was already the next morning and time for her to go to work at the factory. There was no end to her misery.

My father used to say that only in America could you reinvent yourself. Morons become presidents, fools become princes, bandits become CEOs, whores become first ladies. Of course, what he was really getting at was that my uncle, the "immoral two-bit, four-legged thug sodomist" became a millionaire restauranteur overnight. The "golden mountain dream" had eluded my father. The great lories of gold had passed him by, and all he had left in his wretched soul was rage and envy.

My father loved to bitch and mutter and spit his venom into the giant wok of chop suey—into that great noxious swill they called Suburban Chinese American food. He would spit and swear, "Your Mother's cunt! Your turtle's eggs. Your dead bag of dead girl bones!" He would shovel and toss unidentified chunks of flesh and veggies into his giant sizzling wok. An unfiltered Lucky Strike dangling from his lips, rivers of sweat pouring from his greasy hair. I can still see him now, bless his dead soul, red-faced, shoveling and wokking in the great cauldron of hell, hacking and coughing up bile from his black lungs.

So on that fine, succulent spring morning in 1985, I stood in front of the mirror of my own enlightenment. After my initial shock and strange shiver of delight, I noticed that the extra epicanthic folds had made deep creases around the sockets. My eyes felt dry, I supposed, because more surface was now exposed to light. Suddenly, it occurred to me that my new eyes were not beautiful. They looked like they were in a persistent state of alarm. If my cousin had purchased the subtle "Madonna" job at the premium price, I must have had the bargain-basement "Betty Boop."

Finally, I managed to pull myself away from the mirror to go downstairs—to ask my wise sister, Moonie, for her opinion. She said, barely looking up from her cereal, "Nah, don't worry about it. It's the process of assimilation. Happens to the best of us." To me, my sister was God. Like my grandmother, she always had this "Buddhistic" attitude, like, "So what, you turned into a donkey, you'll get over it." She was never a team player. In fact, as a child she was always relegated to the sidelines to warm the bench. The white kids never chose her to play in their team sports. They used to tease her for being a four-eyed geek, and she didn't give a damn. "Dodgeball, what kind a game is that? Who wants to be a moving target and get brain-damaged?"

Moonie was one of those Chinese wise-women who could climb to the apex of a mountain and see everything. Someday she will become a famous biologist or anthropologist, and the people will pay two hundred bucks a plate to hear her talk about neo-genetic theory. And she will get back at those white folks for all those years of humiliation and bench-warming by saying something utterly inane, like, "Caucasoids have more hair on their bodies because they are less evolved," and everybody will applaud, buy her book and stand in a long line for her autograph. Afterward, they will go home and say, "I have touched the sleeve of genius."

But I was not as self-assured as Moonie. I was a shallow nobody. I was a teenager, for God's sake; I didn't have any depth. It was not my station in life to see beyond my petty, personal predicament. I was always falling through the cracks, always afraid of being different. In this way, I was more like Sunny than Moonie. I wanted to fit in. I wanted to be conventional. I wanted the sublime, banal package made in the mall. I wanted to be the perfect, stupid blonde girl who married the perfect stupid, blond boy next door. It was no secret that I wanted to be white, to be "accepted" by the in-crowd, to look as white as a magazine cover—I confess, in sixth grade, in the shameful privacy of my own bathroom, I used to tape my eyelids up with strong Scotch mailing tape and pretend that I was Madonna, with big round cow eyes.

Don't worry. This is no Kafkaesque tale in which I turn into a giant cockroach and my family, the Philistines, beat me up and kill me. I had no fear of my present transformation. We know that anything can happen during adolescence: nipples turn into breasts, breasts turn into beards. Look, there is no mystery to this—at fifteen, the entire female population of the species is mired in self-hatred and most girls despise their own face and body. We all wanted to be cookie-cutter Barbies. If the dominant race had green skin and purple genitals, I would've wanted that too. It was not until I turned thirty-five that I finally realized that I was a beautiful Chinese woman and that my ancient features were hand-painted on the elegant Sung Dynasty scrolls. But so what, my enlightenment came too late; my self-esteem was already irreversibly damaged.

Finally, on that fateful day, Moonie suggested that I tell an adult. Mind you, this was the last resort. In my household, my father was already dead. My mother and grandmother were my guardians now. My mother was doing double shifts at an electronics firm, putting tiny chips into "motherboards." She had just returned to work after spending three days in the hospital recovering from carpal tunnel surgery. And she was asleep, which was her favorite thing to do on Saturdays. I dared not disturb her dreams. She smiled in her sleep. I knew that it was only in her dreams that she could be happy.

So, I had to tell my grandmother, the Great Matriarch. She was the one who raised us while my parents spent most of their lives grueling at their respective sweatshops. She was, as all Chinese grandmothers are, the self-appointed keeper of our Chinese identity. She thought that we were still sojourners, that sooner or later we would improve our Cantonese and pack up our belongings, and that the Chinese from ten thousand diasporas would fly back to China like a pack of homeward geese, back to the Middle Kingdom. And there we would start over in a new Utopian village, marry yellow husbands, produce yellow children and live in eternal golden harmony.

Indeed, my grandmother would be the one to offer me a profound explanation. She was the one who knew about the transmogrification of the soul. She used to tell us stories about all kinds of magical transformations—women turned into foxes, foxes into spirits. Don't be a jerk in this life, for you would be punished in the next by being transformed into a water-rat. She showed us pictures of a Buddhist hell where the punishment always fit the crime. If you were a liar, an ox-headed hatchet man would cut off your tongue. If you were a thief, he would cut off your hands. If you were an adulterer, he would cut off your "you know what." What, then, would be the appropriate punishment for a girlchild who wished so hard to be accepted by white people that her beautiful slanted eyes turned round?

Right then Grandmother was asleep, snoring in her favorite armchair. See that squished gnat on her dress—that was her characteristic signature. The Great Matriarch did not believe in frivolity. I never approached her with the various hormonal problems of prepubescent girls. When I found a spot of blood on my panties, it was Moonie who bought me a copy of Our Bodies, Ourselves and said, "Damn, sorry, sis, but you've entered the world of womanhood."

When two bullies at school beat me up and stole my lunch money, I was too ashamed to tell my grandmother. Instead, I worked an extra shift at my uncle's restaurant and peeled shrimp to pay for the missing money, and I had to work extra hours to pay for my own lunch. I peeled so much shrimp that my allergic fingers blew up like pink pork sausages. Finally, I told my pugilistic father. He immediately took time off from work and drove me to the hospital to get my fingers drained. They also gave me adrenaline shots that made me dizzy. My father then went to school and grabbed my vice principal, Mr. Comely, by his lapels and loudly urged in broken English that those boys be suspended. "Moogoogaipan, you want Moogoogaipan? You get Moogoogaipan." For some reason, my father just happened to have a giant spatula in his pocket that day. He pulled it out and started slapping Mr. Comely with it, making tiny red marks the size of chop-suey chunks all over his face. And there I was, a typical stupid teenager, not proud that my father was trying to defend me, but embarrassed that my geek-father would actually use a spatula as a deadly weapon. It would be a different story had he brandished a machete or a sawed-off assault rifle. What a sight, my father waving his spatula and Mr. Comely backing up, defending himself with a wooden chair and his gold Cross pen.

The boys were never suspended. But suddenly, I was given a reprieve. After all, it's not divine intervention but fate that is the catalyst for change. Within the next few months, everybody sort of—*poof*—disappeared. My father died shortly after that episode; my mother finally gave up on the American dream and bought a one-way ticket back to Hong Kong. Mr. Comely was transferred because of his alcoholism; one bully went to prison; the other moved to Pittsburgh with his divorced mother. (And who could've predicted that I would someday end up graduating magna cum laude from Harvard Law School to become a Yuppie trial attorney for the Small Business Administration? Or that after several failed marriages, I would marry a Filipino activist I met at a coffee shop, a man whose radical ideas would transform my whole life? Or that I would end up devoting my life's work to writing poetry and defending the wives of assassinated guerrillas in Luzon? Of course, this is another story.)

Well, anyway, in my terrible childhood, life was humiliation after humiliation and tiptoeing around that sleeping mother and grandmother. My grandmother had survived a series of natural and man-made disasters: the Sino-Japanese War, famine, drought, flood, torrential rain, bloodthirsty warlords, the Nationalist debacle, Communist tyranny, even a long bout of the cholera epidemic. Now that she was eighty-five and had survived everything and reached the shores of safety, it was the ripe time for her to finally enjoy peace, her grandchildren and napping in her favorite armchair. I was worried that she would have a heart attack upon seeing me. I climbed up onto her lofty lap and said, "Granny, look what happened to my eyes, they've turned round, I am sorry for having been remiss, for being a bad child. For wishing the unthinkable. For dreaming the unmentionable."

She looked at me with her complacent Buddha smile. "So, girlchild, now you are a round-eye. When you were born you were such a beautiful princess, more beautiful than Yang Kuei Fei. You had skin of jade and slanted moon-like eyes. Our ancestors were proud to behold such a plum blossom. Now, look what has happened to you, my little snake-in-the-grass, my little damselfly, how you have changed."

Her compassionate words touched me deeply and I began to cry from my little round eyes. The tears were especially bulbous and fat. She caressed me all night long, telling me ancient revenge tales and fables, where the tiniest girl always ended up victorious. We munched on baggies of glazed ginger and dried plums. No mention was made of my transformation. Deep in her heart, she knew that each step backward would only mean regret—the vector goes in only one direction, the homing geese must find their new nest, the ten thousand diasporas will never coagulate—there was no way back to the Middle Kingdom.

Parable of the Cake

The Neighborwoman said to us, "I'll give you a big cake, little Chinese girls, if you come to the Christmas service with me and accept Jesus Christ, our lord, into your heart." We said, "Okay," and drove with her to the other side of the city and sat through a boring sermon when we should have taken the bus to Chinatown for our Cantonese lessons. Afterward, she gave us a big cake that said "Happy Birthday, Buny" on it. She must have got it for half price because of the misspelling. My sister and I were really hungry after the long sermon, so we gulped down the whole cake as soon as we got home. I got sick and barfed all over the bathroom and my sister had to clean it up before Granny got home. Then my face swelled up for two days on account of my being allergic to the peanut butter in the frosting. My sister was so afraid that I would croak that she confessed everything to Granny. First, Granny gave me some putrid herbal medicine, then she whipped us with her bamboo duster. She whipped us so hard that we both had red marks all over our legs. Then she made us kneel before the Great Buddha for two hours balancing teapots on our heads.

On Christmas Eve, Granny went to Safeway and bought a big

white cake with Santa's face on it and made us go with her to the Neighborwoman's house. She placed the cake into the woman's hands and said to me, "Peapod, translate this, 'Malignant Nun, we do not beg for your God.'" I didn't know how to translate "malignant" and said politely, "Dear Missus, No beg, No God."

My sister and I both wept silently, embarrassed that Granny made us into a spectacle and ashamed that we had to lie to get out of it. Meanwhile, Granny was satisfied that we learned our lesson and decided to take her two favorite peapods to Chinatown for sweet bean dessert. We were the only riders on the bus that night; everybody else was probably home with their families preparing for a big meal. "Merry Christmas, ho ho ho, I am Santa's helper!" said the bus driver. He was wearing a green elf's hat, but we knew that he was really Mr. Rogers the black bus driver. He winked at Granny and gave us each two little candy canes. Granny scowled, "Tsk, tsk, ancient warrior in a fool's cap!" Then we sat way in the back of the bus and Granny began singing our favorite song.

"We will go home and eat cakies, little lotus-filled cakies," Granny sang. "We will eat sweet buns, sweet custard sweet buns!" she sang. "We will eat turnip squares, salty white turnip squares," she sang. "We will eat grass jelly, tangy green grass jelly. We will eat dumplings, soft, steamy dumplings." She was so jolly that we forgot our embarrassing episode and we sang with her, clapping hands—we sang and sang.

Granny would die a few years later, leaving us three thousand dollars under her mattress and a brand new cleaver, still wrapped in Chinese newspaper from Hong Kong. We would grow up into beautiful, clear-skinned young women. We would become born-again Christians and get a complete makeover at the mall. We would work hard in our studies, become successful and drive little white Mercedes. We would remember nothing, nada, nothing that our grandmother taught us. We would learn nothing from our poverty, but to avoid poverty at all cost.

Fa la la la la, little cakies, little cakies, little cakies . . . We would drive around in our little white Mercedes all over southern California eating little cakies. Yes, let's put on the Ritz, sisters: little petit fours in pastels and rainbows . . . booze-soaked baba au rhums, oooh yes, nuttynutty Florentines on little white doilies . . . Oh sisters! Let's ghetto it! Ho Hos, Ding Dongs, pink and white snowballs, let's suck the creamy hearts out of the Twinkies. Come hither, come yon, young Chinese girls. Come, let's drive around in our little white Mercedes eating cakies, little cakies. Come, let the crumbs fall down our chins and dance on our laps. Come, light light airy madeleines, come, creamy creamy trifles. Come, little cakies, little cakies. Come, the sweet, sweet hereafter. . . .

Parable of the Fish

G randmother, how do you know that the fish are happy?"

"Irreverent polyp-of-a-child, how do you know that I don't know that the fish are happy?"

"Well, Grandmother, you're not a fish. You cannot know what fish know."

"Well, my ignorant gnat-of-a-girl, you are not I, how do you know that I don't know what fish know."

. . .

One day she fetched me from school and said, "Let's take a stroll through our honorable Mayor Willie Brown's mansion. *The Gold Mountain News* said that he wants all of his citizens to visit his new Japanese water garden." So we took the No. 25 bus and transferred to a No. 85 bus at the Montgomery station, where she bought me a cold can of Coke from a machine. I knew that it was going to be a special day.

When we got to the mansion, we went straight to the Mayor's new water garden. There were pink and white lotuses in bloom, assorted duckweed and hyacinth. Catkins and dwarf willows bent over; they looked like they were washing their beautiful hair in the pond. Suddenly, without warning, my grandmother stuck her hand into our honorable Mayor's fish pond and pulled out a magnificent spotted orange carp. It was at least three feet long and as it thrashed, its brilliant scales shimmered like mirrors. She pulled her smile into a deep frown then pointed to the bronze plaque on the wall that said in both Chinese and English, "A gift to the city of San Francisco from His Majesty the Emperor Hirohito of Japan."

She then said, "Remember this, my mooncake, Hirohito was a mass murderer and rapist and this pond was built with Chinese blood." So she swung the fish by the tail and whacked it five times against the stone wall. When it continued to thrash and convulse, she took her trusty cleaver from her giant purse and whacked it five more times with the blunt edge. "This one for Manchuria, this one for Nanking, this for our cousin Lu, this for Auntie Jade . . ." When it finally stopped thrashing, she wrapped it up in newspaper and stuffed it in her purse; and we walked briskly past the guard station toward the bus stop. The guard was listening to some funky tune in his earphones and didn't even notice us.

So we took it home on the No. 4 bus to Market Street, where we changed to a No. 65 bus back to the Richmond. On the bus we met her skinny gossipy fussbudget friend, who always wore an ugly hairnet. They started talking in this ancient dialect about Mr. Hong's whore-mongering son. What a pity that the whole regal bloodline has been tainted by this whore-mongering bastard. The whore-mongering bastard emptied the till of the laundromat and went to Hong Kong to continue his whore-mongering activities. Then they went on about Mrs. Lew's slut-of-a-dead-girl. That slut-of-a-dead-girl went on to live with several white devils. They said she lived with three of them at one time. One devil lived in the Richmond, one lived in Mill Valley, one in San Jose. That she was always driving and stopping and leaving her grandmother in the back seat to bake in the sun. Then my grandmother turned to me and said, "You better not do that to me when you get older."

They rattled on like two ancient kettles. There was a mother-beating gangster named Wu. An ox-naped gigolo named Lee. A long-spined good-for-nothing named Fu . . . "Oh, how ironic that he was named Fu! Ha, ha!" A cockroach-eating numb-skull named Ming. A mutton-of-a-loser named Wei. How can Buddha visit such terrible creatures upon us?

I said I had to pee and Grandmother said, "Hush, you should have peed in the green plastic toilets in the Mayor's house. Did you know that it took him two weeks to install those plastic toilets for his loving citizens?"

When we got home, she wasted no time to clean the fish and steamed it with ginger and onions, and ordered me to climb up the back fire escape and pluck fresh spinach from our communal roof garden. "Pull out the whole root," she said. "You must leave room for the baby shoots."

"Tonight is a special celebration," she said. She presented the magnificent orange carp on a large celadon plate that her own grandmother had given her. She shaped the spinach into curly tidal waves all around the lip of the giant plate. She decorated the fish and capped the spinach waves with bits of candied ginger; they shimmered like diamonds. And look! The fish is wearing a pearly onion necklace! I squealed with joy as I collected the sweet gems and saved them in a little dish for later, when I would relish them as a late snack with fruit and tea.

. . .

"So you ungrateful, arrogant drop-plum, tell me that the fish aren't happy!" This time, I could not formulate an argument, for my mouth was already busy sucking on a fin. The inner fleshy side was especially tasty. "I must tell you, my little trinket, my hungry little glowworm, that I have no doubts, heaven has issued an edict: I know that the fish are capable of sublime happiness."

Parable of Squab

When Sasha moved to New Jersey, he bequeathed his whole collection of pigeons to Mei Ling and Moonie. Since they all lived in the same building, it was easy for Sasha to give them the keys to the rooftop coop and say, "They're all yours, suckers!" By year end, there were 155 birds and counting. The girls could identify each of the birds by their markings and had renamed them after flowers and famous women.

There was Dandelion, Iris, Fleabane, Peony, Jonquil . . . Tiger-lily had fancy horizontal stripes on her wings . . . Jackie, Eleanor, Madonna, Lilith . . . Anna Akhmatova was an especially beautiful bird, with long lashes and blue, sultry eyes. Each time a new chick hatched, the girls would go to the library and search through both the *Encyclopedia of Famous Women* and *The Sunset Almanac of Wildflowers* for a new name.

They fed the birds breadcrumbs from Zack's bakery. After school, they helped Zack sweep his street front in exchange for all the leftover bread. They also brought home scraps and day-old rice from the Double Happiness, their family restaurant.

At first, their Grandmother Wong was not opposed to this hobby because it did not cost the family anything and because it kept the girls home after school instead of playing ball with Sven and Lem or banging on their guitars with Igor and Ivor in the neighborhood garage band. Or ruining their pretty complexions in the late afternoon sun skateboarding and break-dancing with Julio and Coolio. To their grandmother's dismay, the neighborhood was rife with rambunctious twins since the onset of fertility drugs, which meant that Mei Ling and Moonie had too many opportunities to get into mischief.

One day, for a variety of reasons, this pigeon hobby became a nuisance in the grandmother's eyes. Perhaps the Matriarch was tired of the girls bringing feathers home on their clothes. There were flying wisps everywhere. She also had the suspicion that the girls were not doing their homework in the library, but spending most of their time culling names for the chicks. Furthermore, the Great Matriarch started thinking about the idea of raising animals not for food but for entertainment, and her proletariat instincts came back to her. She was worried that the girls were getting lax in their work ethic. Breeding pigeons for fun is not a worthy working-class pastime: it's a bourgeois vanity sport. This was a remnant of corrupt feudalism, she thought, where crickets, trapped in quaint bamboo cages, sang for their supper like catamites . . . where desperate parents raised young girls for the flesh trade . . . where fat colorful carp decorated the huge elaborate moats in the imperial gardens while the masses starved at the palace gate.

And in this decadent era of late American capitalism, she saw the diners at the restaurant appear with their lapdogs, groomed and pedicured, while the homeless rummaged through the restaurant garbage cans after midnight. One fat red-faced man, who drove a Rolls-Royce, carried his yapping Chihuahua under his coat and fed him like a baby. He always ordered Peking duck for the dog and the ghastly sweet and sour pork for himself. The cooks would throw in extra sugar and grease in the godawful recipe to please him. As the years went by, Grandmother Wong watched both the man and the little dog get fatter and fatter until both had to get quadruple bypass surgery.

She noticed that the neighborhood cats would give birth to more cats—fat, clawless mutants—meaningless creatures, raised not to catch mice but to purr beneath the table. They've forgotten their role in the order of things. The stealthy king of the jungle, top-of-the-food-chain monster, was now a disgrace to its race. It could never return to the jungle and face its relatives.

One day, Grandmother Wong had this great idea. The restaurant was about to have a wedding party for the son of a local Chinatown merchant. She was told that this son loved squab. She thought that a perfect dragon and phoenix dish would be minced squab and oyster in lettuce cups. So she decided that when the girls were in school, she would go up on the roof with a large net and capture some of the birds while they slept in their giant cage. Squab was expensive these days. She thought about the money she would save by slaughtering the captive birds instead of buying dozens of them from a local farmer. Finally, these birds would be useful and contribute to the economy of the people.

When she got to the rooftop though, they all flew away in one wing-flapping fury. They acted as if they knew what she was up to. And they stayed away for weeks. The old lady was angry at their outsmarting her. Finally, she told the girls to call them. She said, "Summon them to me. I want to query them." Mei Ling gave her secret call and Moonie blew into her silent whistle. But the pigeons didn't come. Mei Ling said, "Grandmother, you always told us that Buddha knows our bad intentions. Perhaps the pigeons are the souls of the Buddha and they know that you have bad intentions."

Suddenly, the Matriarch felt ashamed and sang a verse:

What flower yearns to be mulch
What pigeon wants to be minced

She decided that these were very wise and virtuous pigeons. And like herself they were survivors and were probably exiles from a distant land. Their ancestors suffered both natural and man-made disasters: horrific, bloody world wars; long seasons of drought and famine; clear-cut deforestation; the atom bomb; powerful pesticides; and even bourgeois pleasure shooting. And besides, they were born hated creatures. People were prejudiced against them and despised them for no reason. It was a kind of racism! She decided after much thought that these birds deserved a long life.

She let them return and thrive on the rooftop, and when the girls went away to college, she would go up to the roof and hand-feed them herself. Two days before her ninety-fifth birthday, she was found dead on the roof . . . she was in the midst of feeding the birds a New Year's treat of sunflower seeds that she roasted in peanut oil. She fell asleep among them and never woke up. Moonie and Mei Ling, who both grew up into fine ambitious women with careers and families of their own, and who no longer had the time or the interest in keeping the birds, decided to set them free.

Meanwhile, a new wave of immigrants moved into the neighborhood. A Thai Laotian family named Chinalai moved into the Wong apartment. The Gonzalez family now lives in Sasha's apartment but with a set of rambunctious teenage quadruplet girls! But the tale of Grandmother Wong's magnificent pigeons lives on in the children's imaginations. And to this day, when young kids in the neighborhood see a group of pigeons flying high in a kindred flock, they point up and say, "There they go, Grandmother Wong's pigeons, they're looking for her in paradise."

Monologue: Grandmother Wong's New Year Blessings

OR, THEY CAN'T KILL US IF THEY

DON'T KNOW OUR NAMES

In memory of Isabel Alvarez Razo (1914–2008)

I say, Moonie, you drive me to my friend's house. Mei Ling, you come to translate. Mei Ling say, but Granny, I writing paper on *Moby Dick*. Moonie say, I memorizing Declaration of Independence for speech class.

I say, *Moby Dick*? No worry, big fish story. Chinese girl have good memory: life, liberty, hirsute happiness. Easy. We go to my friend's house. Give them New Year presents. We do every year. If we don't, for all year, we have bad luck. You too stupid, you don't know about this.

Moonie say, don't call us stupid. That's child abuse.

I say, okay smart turtle egg, call big lawyer put me in jail. Forget it, I don't need you drive me. I go a hundred buses, two hundred transfers. I walk ten thousand miles!

. . .

They good girls, do homework, get straight As. But I have to teach respect. Only I do, because their mother and father too busy make money. They open restaurant at 4 a.m. Go to sleep at one. They get three-hour sleep. All my son do is swear . . . fuck this, fuck that . . . and Mei Ling mother, all she do is cry . . . She say, I go back to Hong Kong! I go back to Hong Kong! In Hong Kong she use to ride rickshaw to teahouse. Now, in America, she work like slave. Her hand use to be white and soft. Now rough like sea cucumber. I say, don't you know? This what you suppose to do in America? Work day and night. You think Jesus or Buddha give you free money? All they do work work for money then fight fight about money. Money never enough. They always keep big eyes on cash register. I say, your daughters grow breasts! You can't see? You don't care, grow breasts or snakes!

Little peapods, I say, you don't want to be like that. You get straight As, go work high in the sky in glass building, be king of office. Lawyer, doctor, president, I don't care, close restaurant if you want, just don't dance at Pink Pussycat. I don't want you cook if you don't want cook. My Moonie hates to cook. And I say that's okay. She won't get husband, but who needs husband, end up like my son, useless, spit in wok, hate this, hate that.

. . .

So we load up presents in van. Drive and drive. Moonie say, Granny, we're lost, where we going? I say, what the matter, you suppose to know your way. We drive in circles. Don't you know the way to black town?

Mei Ling say, not black town, Grandma, don't you know, not

political correct to say "black town"? Say, Watts. Say, Little Sudan. Say, hood. Say, crib. Don't say, black town.

Chinatown, black town, yellow town, brown town, white town, I only speak truth. What color people in this neighborhood, you tell me. Not white people. White people won't live here. They live up white people hill where white people live.

Moonie say, I don't like to go to Mrs. Faith house, she always cry. I say, silly piglet. She always cry because she has sad story: You know why she here? Salama and Bobo parents were killed by Janjaweed. Don't you know Janjaweed? So, if she cry, she has something to cry about, not like you cry because you skateboarding with Coolio and break your tooth.

Mei Ling say, why don't she move? She lives next to giant power station. Mrs. Roberts science teacher say it cause cancer. I say, don't say cancer, unlucky, it's New Year. Mrs. Faith too poor to move. Spoiled girl, you give her million dollars. Then she move.

. . .

Mrs. Faith grandbaby Salama is shy, watch behind curtain with thumb in mouth. I say, girls, go play with Salama, I want to talk to Mrs. Faith. She open door in bright purple dress with yellow flowers on it. She laughs and she cries loud and give me big hug with big breasts.

She say, here I am, twilight of life, suppose to lie in big pillow chair, watch lions dance; instead, I watch grand babies . . . day, night, we never safe. I say, Mrs Faith, Janjaweed can't kill your grandbabies, you in America now. She say, I worry, nightmare every night, can't sleep, carry big machete. I tell Moonie, bring my bag, and I pull out big China cleaver. I say, this better than big machete. It's biggest cleaver . . . I tell Auntie Wu to buy. Auntie Wu say there's no bigger cleaver in China.

She smells it, kiss blade and say, thank you, Mrs. Wong, I can kill lion and twenty hyenas. I say, yes, you chop chop Janjaweed, lion, hyenas, demons—boil in big soup. Eat for New Year. Nobody bother you.

I say, I pray to great Buddha that your grandson don't become gangster. Mrs. Faith say, I pray to Jesus your girls don't dance at Pink Pussycat. She give me a big necklace, string of big orange beads. I say, thank you, I think it's ugly, but I will wear all New Year week. Then, she give me big dish of goat. I say, goat, I hate goat . . . it taste too strong. She say, it suppose to be strong, like how God will it. I say, okay, I give to Mei Ling. She love goat.

She give me big breast hug and not let me go. She has big strong arms. I say 2008 will be good year. It's Rat year. Rats will come out to play and kill the mean cat. I promise, I say. She cry, laugh, cry, and kiss me goodbye.

• • •

Then, we stop for gas, so Mei Ling get Diet Coke. I say, you thirsty for eating too much goat. Hurry, we go Mrs. Gonzalez house in Mexican town. Mei Ling say, bar-ri-o, we going to bar-ri-o, Granny. Moonie say, I hope Mrs. Gonzalez don't cry too; old ladies cry, yuk, gross! I'm tired of old lady crying.

We go to Mrs. Gonzalez house. We have to climb four flights of stairs. Moonie complain because I make her carry two big jugs. What's in these things, she say, they weigh a ton! I say, don't complain, you have strong shoulder from kung fu. Good practice to carry.

Mrs. Gonzalez shout from upstairs, Señora, Señora Wong! I hear her fast walk. I tell Mei Ling to translate, "Don't walk down, we come up, don't hurt lumbago!" (No-anda-abajo-señora. Subimos-ahora. No-ofende-su-lumbago, por-favor!)

I tell her many years to move in apartment downstairs and she say, no, addicts crawl through window. I say, put wire around window then make wire in plug. Moonie know how. Moonie genius with electricity, got first prize in science fair. She fry him like chicken. Mrs. Gonzalez say, no, that's illegal and not nice. I say, why be nice to drug addict? They nice to you?

Look at cute, fatty Gonzalez girls. How you pronounce name, Mei Ling. She say, So-phi-a, Sa-bin-a, Sol-e-dad, Se-ren-a. They are little dolls. Pigtails. Fluffy dress. Like little cakes. Who spend hours curling pigtails and fluffing up dresses and put bows in hair? Their grandmother Maria Gonzalez, not their mother, Maria Romero. Their mother, Maria Romero, work all morning waitress at the Big Sombrero Restaurant, then, work at Hilton in afternoon as receptionist; all night she go college to become accountant. She good with numbers, I say to Moonie. Hardworking, good with numbers and you get good future.

Mrs. Gonzalez bring us em-pan-ad-as. I say, Mei Ling slow down with translation. I can't pronounce. She say, oh just call them Mexican dumplings. I say, why Mexicans like corn more than rice. Mrs. Gonzalez say, we like corn, rice and beans like one perfect family, father son and holy spirit. I say, I don't understand bean, it taste dirty, maybe I put soy sauce and garlic or maybe I put sugar . . . make sweet bean paste.

We laugh and laugh . . . she say, why you have good skin for old lady. Mei Ling translates and roll eyeballs. I say, my secret, I bring umbrella everywhere I go, rain or shine, I don't want get wrinkled or too dark. She say, yes, everybody want be white face lady, no matter Mexican or Chinese . . . I too dark, this why husband run away. I say, I too dark, this why husband die heart attack. We laugh and laugh.

Then, she start crying. Hand Moonie a big basket of Mexican

dumplings. She say, there is sweet ones and salty ones. Yam and bean, bean and cactus, Mei Ling translates. I give her big jugs of tiger-bone wine from China. She hit her heart with little fist and cry loud, Mrs. Wong, estoy-consada, estoy-consada, estoy-consada! I hit heart, cry with her, I estoy-consada, too!

· · ·

In car, Mei Ling say, Granny, you give her tiger-bone wine. It's 100 proof. Like drinking fire. I say, mind your business, little worm— she need fire to keep her heart burning. Don't you know she wake up at three, make one thousand Mexican dumplings to sell at market. You don't see dumplings all over kitchen? We old, but we need take care of grandbabies and make money. We never sleep. What will happen when all grandmas run out of fire? We can't die. We die, nobody take care of you.

Mei Ling shut up. Then, we drive up the hill to rich people houses. Every New Year, I bring phoenix web to Mrs. Goldstein, and I bring her extra sauce on side. Moonie say, Mrs. Goldstein is your BFF because she likes to suck bones out loud then spit them on floor like Chinese. I say, she no spit on floor, she ladylike and spit in napkin. Moonie say, we don't like Benny, all he do is sit in closet, play dungeon and dragon. Mei Ling say, yes, he strange, he talk to nobody. He'll grow up, become shooter.

Mrs. Goldstein say, phoenix web not salty enough this time, Mrs. Wong. I say, Benny's Grandmother, I should bring pork ears, they're crunchy and more salty. She say, we Jewish and can't eat pork ears . . . how about ox ears? I say, ox ear no taste good . . . but ox intestines taste good with curry and scallion. She say, why you call phoenix web; are they really made of phoenix? I say, no they not made of phoenix, funny lady, no such thing phoenix, but we Chinese try make sound better, "phoenix web" sound better than "duck web," no? She say, no, you must tell TRUTH; people expect phoenix and get duck. Mei Ling say, enough chicken and duck debate . . . you old ladies think you're Plato!

Then, I say, speaking TRUTH, what happen to Benny's parents? Why Benny living with you? Divorce, she say, my son left good wife and married shiksa. I ask Moonie, what is shiksa? She say, the yellow-hair bimbo, you saw them kissy at restaurant remember? I say, that shiksa! I say, men too stupid, my boy like gamble, yours like shiksa.

Then we talking about Germans and Japanese . . . Moonie say, oh, no, here come ancient history lesson. Make it short, Granny! I say, Chinese proverb "Small nation like small men with big ambition." She say, they killed six million of us. I say, I guess twenty million of us. She say, like killing cockroach, like killing lice. I say, cockroach, lice, we okay, we survived! What is killing American children? she say. Too greedy, I say, stomach bigger than brain. She say, my son not wise, he like money and shiksa more than Benny. I hear her son, Mr. Goldstein, in back room yelling into phone.

She say, I have bad news, Mrs. Wong, I have cancer, not long to live . . . Will you remember to watch Benny, make sure he does homework? She give me white envelope with words "Open When I'm Gone." I say, you not die, don't say that on New Year, bad luck. I hate white envelope: it means immigration lawyer and funeral. Always bad news. Then, she give girls big gold box of Godiva chocolate. Mei Ling claps. Moonie jump up down like monkey. I say, not polite! I pinch, make her stop.

In car, Mei Ling say Mrs. Goldstein survive Buchenwald— we study Holocaust and went to survivors' museum on field trip . . . she real survivor. I say, she survive Holocaust, but will die of broken heart. Because her son like shiksa and money and don't take care of Benny.

. . .

We run out of New Year presents. Mei Ling say, can we go home now? All this old lady stuff depressing. Moonie say, I won't grow old. I commit suicide before forty, so I won't have to grow old. Mei Ling say, you give me rat poison, kill me first when I'm thirty-nine so you can suicide at forty. Moonie say, cyanide pill faster, we use cyanide pills. Then they rip up big box of chocolate and stuff mouths.

I say, go home and memorize "life, liberty, and hirsute happiness." Read *Moby Dick*. Someday, you open eyes, TRUTH not in books, stupid girl poop!

Moonie say, you not suppose to say stupid no more. Say "in-tel-lect-ual-ly challenged."

They put on earphones, eat chocolates and pretend I'm not in car. I don't care, I talk loud. I talk to ghosts.

Mrs. Gonzalez, when you die, I burn incense and little pink dumplings and pretty ribbons so you have something good to eat, and you can put bows on all dead children in heaven. I also send tiger-bone wine. You drink, breathe fire like dragon, barbeque bad people who crawl through window.

Mrs. Faith, when you die I burn ten thousand paper cleavers. Janjaweed ghost won't kill you, you kill them first. Chop off their heads. Cut up their livers. Stir-fry in big wok. Then, you have peace in heaven.

Mrs. Benny Grandmother, when you die, I burn phoenix web for you, almond cookies, veggie eggroll, all your favorite food . . . Then, I burn ten thousand soldiers of Qin. They knee down with magic bow and arrow, they protect you. Nobody hurt you, no Germans, no Japanese.

I write names of all our grandbabies: Mei Ling, Moonie, Benny, Salama, Bobo, So-phi-a, Sa-bin-a, Sol-e-dad, Se-ren-a. See girls, I can pronounce, I write on red paper, then burn them, make names—*poof*—all smoke. Girls, grandbabies, study hard, make happy life. No worry, demons can't kill you if they don't know your names!

Ax Handle

Grandmother comes to Mei Ling in a dream. *There is a mosquito on my nose. It spins around my head and it bites me on the tip of my nose, over and over again. You might think that it is a trifle. But it shall buzz in my ear and annoy me to all eternity. Do you know how it feels to be annoyed to all eternity? It's like your Auntie Wu's high-pitched voice buzzing at your ear about real estate and junk bonds . . . that's what it's like. You were my favorite peapod. Remember, I used to carry you on my back and sang you ancient lullabies. When you had that long fever, I cradled you up and down Cat Street. Remember how I yelled at the prostitutes, "My Mei Ling is going to be somebody; she's going to America!" And they yelled back, "Look at her, sickly, coughing, she's rat turd; she'll amount to nothing!" And remember, I picked up a big piece of kohlrabi from my bag and hurled it and knocked the pimp out, put him in a coma? Remember that? They dared to upset a proud grandmother! Please, little Mei Ling, take your merciful ax and kill this mosquito, so that I can rest in peace.*

So Mei Ling throws the ax and it spins three perfect revolutions, bisecting the mosquito while still buzzing on her grandmother's nose. Her grandmother praises her accuracy. *It was I who taught you to be focused.* Her apparition slithers back into the dark earth and is quelled for ten thousand years.

The next day, Mei Ling's dead husband appears in her dream. *Look, Mei Ling, this aggravating maggot. It squirms and writhes and it crawls in and out of my nostrils and eyeholes. It is giving me a headache. It will not give me peace. Can you imagine having an eternal itch that you can't scratch? Right now, it is resting on my nose, taking a short respite, I suppose. Please take your merciful ax and remove it for me. Remember, love-a-dove, how we used to watch TV together and Seinfeld, my favorite show? You hated it but sat with me anyway and said, "They're such meaningless, ridiculous, self-centered fools." You continued to read poetry. Remember, how sweet it was. I would watch TV and laugh out loud. You would wear earphones and listen to endless Schubert and read poetry. Each sitting on our respective side of the couch. Those were the days of marital harmony, weren't they? Hunnybunny, don't you remember how smooth and lovely it was?*

Mei Ling ponders for a moment, then throws the ax; it turns two revolutions and clips off her dead husband's head. He yells (well, the head on the ground yells), *You stupid bitch, now my ghost will roam the underworld, headless and unrepentant for ten thousand years!*

· · ·

So goes the story about using the ax to make the ax handle. Staring at the original design for too long might make you crazy: the model too close at hand. And that unforgiving muse, who believes that she can shave the fine distinctions between she who really loved you with unconditional maternal clarity; who shared her last grain of rice with you in the refugee boat; who fanned you all night long with an old *Life* magazine to keep your brain from boiling in the killer Hong Kong heat; who, on her eighty-second year, waited patiently outside the exam room with an open bottle of Coke and three tiny mooncakes to celebrate your acing your LSATs . . . and he who is just going on the existential ride in the hay, cheats on you six to seven times with young bimbos, and expects you not to hold a grudge into his grave . . . Well, the muse takes care of her own, doesn't she? She keeps her soapstone in an oily leather pouch.

2

Oh Lord! Here Come the Double Happiness Twins

I would do what I pleased, and doing what I pleased, I should have my will, and having my will, I should be contented; and when one is contented, there is no more to be desired; and when there is no more to be desired, there is an end of it.

—*Don Quijote*

All who would win joy must share it; happiness was born a twin.

—*Lord Byron*

Oh Lord! Here Come
the Double Happiness
Twins

I.
PICARESQUE TRAVELS

M ei Ling and I are scouting around a glitzy neighborhood in La Jolla, trying to find the only hippy-dippy left-winged Unitarian church in southern California. It's bad enough that we are wearing satin red hapi coats with the restaurant's bright yellow insignia "Double Happiness" embroidered on the back; we are also driving a cherry red van with a picture of a giant fortune cookie on the side, and 570 pounds of eggrolls, cold sesame noodles and sweet and sour pork, you name it, onboard to be delivered. It's a fucking good thing that we don't have to do this often. But it's Christmas Eve. All the delivery boys have the night off with their families. We're back from college for the holidays and our psycho-cleaver-wielding Granny won't let us off the hook. And who ends up driving? Me, of course, because my hormonal limp-wristed girly-girl sister can't drive worth shit.

II.
HIPPIE JESUS

So we finally get to this funky-looking church, which is in fact not in La Jolla but in the back alleys of Pacific Beach. The building's octagonal, made of raw pine wood with knots all showing and a giant messy purple bougainvillea practically blocking the entry. A hippy-dippy-looking dude walks out with beautiful long blond hair and a crown of very gay large daisies around his head.

"Look," Mei Ling says, "it's hippie-dude Jesus!" He snarls at us, then breaks out a cheesy smile from cheek to cheek and says, "Yeah, and look at you two, the Double Happiness twins! I think I've died and gone to heaven!"

"You are just being born, baby Jesus, don't you know your history?" says Mei Ling.

"All right," I say. "It's Christmas Eve, and we all look ridiculous. Take your food and pay us $849, asshole. This includes the ten percent delivery charge."

He pulls out a shiny platinum credit card.

"Who's paying the bill, your daddy, Mr. God?" Mei Ling says, laughing so hard that she clutches her crotch to prevent herself from pissing.

"I'll even give you my fat tip, pretty little Chinese twins."

He pulls out an extra fifty. "Ho, ho, ho, Merry Christmas," he says. "You two must come back in April—Easter eggrolls for when I get crucified."

"Ha, ha, you're so funny. We're tired of your Jesus metaphors already. Do you think you're in a World Lit 101 class or something? Just sign the receipt, Son of Man."

Oh, oh . . . Two balls of fire explode in Mei Ling's eyes. I know that fire. Any minute now, she's going to *gamahuche* the poor dude and it will not be a pretty sight; she'll devour him crowned-with-thorns-head first, and by February she will have spat him out as human waste. He will wander around the earth, naked save his strappy sandals. Once you meet the fiery eyes of Mei Ling, aka Venus-man-trap, love-goddess-slut-sister-super-vixen, you are dead meat!

Before I finish thinking the word "meat" she wags her ass up to Jesus and kisses him smack on the lips. I say, "Oh no, Mei Ling, don't go there. We got a few more deliveries to make. One in the mean Samoan hood. Don't disappear and make me do it all by myself."

Before you know it, they start French-kissing and grinding their pelvises together, so I have no choice but to treat him to a Bruce Lee *Jeet Kun Do* short-angle kick in the shin to make him stop.

"Whoa, little sister," he cries. "Don't kung-fu me now, it's the Nativity." He tries to swing at me, but I block his arm with a Precious-Duck-Swims-Thru-Lotus punch and hit him in the gut. He screams and falls to the ground, then tries to grab my ankle. I leap up and bounce two backward somersaults and nail my landing.

"Ten, ten, ten, a perfect ten," Mei Ling yells.

"Damn, what are you," Jesus says, "some kinda ninja freak?"

"Call me Moonie Mooncake Vixen. I've come to seek revenge against the wrongs perpetuated against my peeps!" I say. "And I wreck phony baloney saviors with Messiah complex perverts like you!"

III.
YOU, TOO, ASSHOLE DUCINEA!
ALOHA, MELE KALIKIMAKA!

I drag Mei Ling away by her ponytail, but she keeps her head wrenched, staring back at him with wild love. "Stop that cock-gazing, Mei Ling!"

We drive our stupid van all over southeast San Diego—the southern California hellhole: billboards in Vietnamese, Chinese, Arabic, and Spanish popping up everywhere and giving me a headache. Prostitutes of all colors and sexual persuasions: one dressed like Cher is wearing a Santa hat and is jabbering with an elf in green hot pants. But it's pretty thinned out tonight. The streets are quiet, as if we were on a Hollywood set on Sunday or awakening to the aftermath of a great atom bomb blast.

"I bet even the most hardcore pimps are at their mommy's house with white napkins on their laps, eating ham dinner," Mei Ling shouts out the window.

"I bet all the pagans, Jews and Hindus, Buddhists, Jains, Sikhs, and atheists are having Christmas dinner," I shout back.

"I bet Hamas, Hezbollah and Al Qaeda are all at home slurping eggnog and opening presents!"

We're the only fools driving around delivering other people's food. And I'm hungrier than hell, so Mei Ling opens up a big box of half-frozen mini mooncakes left over from November. I quickly chisel off the flaky crust with my front teeth and start licking around the lotus paste to reach the yummy eggyolk moon. Mei Ling likes to put the whole cakie into her mouth and suck on it until she gets to the center. She then spits out the yolk. She hates yolks, so she gives them to me . . . the Moonie yolkmeister!

One hand holding a cakie, the other wheeling like a maniac, I almost run over a dumb kid on a skateboard with tattoos oozing from his chin to his asshole.

"We're looking for the Samoan Hawaiian Cultural Center. It's supposed to be on Zapata Street."

"Hell, I dunno," he says. "I'm not Samoan. I'm bonafide Aztec, but I like to fuck twins."

"Well, Mr. Ass-stick, we don't fuck morons," I say to him, flipping him the condor.

I can see now that the Center is two blocks down. The neon's all lit up. We are mesmerized as we drive up, all the island knick-knacks flashing in bright tropical orange and green and pink. The royal palm tree in front is decorated with cool teeny Xmas ornament ukuleles and rubber hula dolls. Beneath the tree is a manger scene with a bare black baby Jesus and Mary, wearing a bright pink muumuu—and surrounded by the obligatory signs "Aloha!" "Reclaim the Homeland, Bruddah!" and "Mele Kalikimaka."

Two aunties, one skinny, one fat, come out and give us two fresh plumeria leis at the backdoor. They kiss us both. Big auntie nearly crushes my bones with a big hug. They have ordered seven hundred dollars' worth of ribs, fried rice, wontons, you name it. Skinny auntie peeks into the giant platters.

"You forgot the Kahlua pig," she says. "Are you kidding?" I start searching in the van, poking into the other packages. "I swear, your pig is here. The chefs stayed up all night and pampered him for you."

Meanwhile, Mei Ling is talking to a huge, beautiful, seven-foot-tall Samoan Hawaiian jock in a bright red Matisse-print sarong-thing. "No, no," I say. "Mei Ling, not again. There's trouble here in paradise. We forgot Kahlua pig."

Before I can say more, she's straddling his shoulders, and he's dancing and whirligigging her around. She is drinking some deadly looking island punch. They're blasting Israel Kamakawiwo'ole singing "Somewhere Over the Rainbow," a bit tear-jerky-sentimental if you ask me.

I grab on to his thigh and bite him hard. He yelps like a big dog and drops Mei Ling like a sack of Alpo. I drag Mei Ling away by her ponytail again.

"We'll be back with the Kahlua pig, Big Dude. Meanwhile put junior back into your skirt."

IV.
THE CURSE OF THE MISSING
KAHLUA PIG

In the van, I slap Mei Ling three times. I shake her five times more: the magic rites force her to snap out of her libidinous trance. Slapping her six times and shaking her nine would be enough to pull her out of a quasi-coma, the procedure only for emergencies when she is totally out of control. If I slap her nine times and rattle her fifteen and she still doesn't snap out of it, that means the chance is lost. We're spending the night, and I'll have to fuck the brother. By the looks of it, she's only on stage two of the pussy-control meter. I can still pry her off. I am proud when I am successful. This gorgeous dude used to be a halfback for the San Diego Chargers. Mind you, this guy was only warming the bench, a cipher on the depth chart, but he could still crush me with one of his body slams!

"Take stock of yourself, sister, we have a long night. We have to go to Romero Electronics yet."

"Have you got hot sauce in your eyes?" she says. "This dude is beautiful."

I say, "Yes, but you're acting like a whore! Do you have to always taste what's in front of you? What if they give you arsenic in a cup of Cherry Garcia ice cream? What if they give you a banana split doused with bubonic plague?"

But smarty-pants says, "What if they give me Brad Pitt dipped in Nutella? What if they give me Will Smith smeared in crushed Oreos and Reese's Peanut Butter Cups? What if they give me Jude Law smothered in Cool Whip? What if they give me Orlando Bloom's elf ears dipped in bright red strawberry syrup from IHOP?" She high-fives me and laughs from her gut.

She says, "What do ya think, I've been locked up in the lab all semester, dissecting cadavers of frogs. I am trapped in an all-girl dorm, and my dorm mate is an ex-Carmelite nun." Then Granny calls us on the cell phone. "What happened? Auntie Skinny called me. She say you forgot Kahlua pig. Kahlua pig swimming in big tub like a baby and you don't see. Come back! Cockroaches! Poopmaggots!" Click.

Back at the restaurant, arms crossed and scowling, Granny's waiting for us with the Kahlua pig. Her eyes are two angry slits, and we are afraid.

"It's Mei Ling's fault," I say. Mei Ling says, "It's Moonie's fault." Granny just stares at us, tapping her foot. She grabs Mei Ling by her ear and twists it down.

"Mei Ling, you stop hot pants. Auntie Skinny says you drink bug juice and dance with nephew. Better you, Moonie, not drive drunk or I'll flay you with big chops." She waves her stainless-steel cleaver.

V.

I TURN TO MY AUDIENCE WITH A BRILLIANT SOLILOQUY, or MY IMMIGRANT DREAM IN A BABY'S SILK SLIPPER

Why am I my sister's keeper? I'm only twelve seconds older. But I am as clean as the white line on the highway: I'm attending Stanford and Mei Ling's at Harvard, both of us on pre-med scholarships and on our ways to becoming important doctors. Mei Ling, the bleeding-heart-liberal girly-girl, wants to be a plastic surgeon for the poor. She wants to make pretty the mangled, the decrepit, the dispossessed. She says it's a political act. It's a kind of "lookism," she says. People who look different are oppressed by perfect-looking Barbie doll types. I say, "Sure, you just want to be a plastic surgeon so that you can make lots of money and give yourself eternal face-lifts. You're a narcissistic bitch."

"You'll see," says Mei Ling. "You will come to me when your tits fall down to your knees." I say, "My tits will never fall down to my knees. I'm in perfect shape." I flex my Wonder Woman breasts. They—*boing*—stick straight out like Athena's bronze shields.

I have it all planned out. I'm not going to do anything too difficult like brain surgery, and I don't have any missionary zeal either. I don't want to go to the jungles of Africa and cure AIDS, malaria, starvation, typhoid, TB, diabetes, cancer, civil war: let the girly-girl tackle those problems. I want to be a cardiologist for the rich and famous by the time I'm twenty-five; I will save my money and quit and become governor of a small state like Rhode Island at thirty-five. I shall gather momentum and become the first Chinese American woman president at fifty. I don't want to become president too early because I want to have a family first. I'll marry a nice quiet husband in the hi-tech field like Mr.

Yang at Yahoo. This way, he will be busy in front of the computer and won't harass me for sex. I'll give birth to a little girl, a "little cute-as-a-button Moon." I'll dress her in Gap jeans and leather jackets. She'll be a mini-me. Then, if they don't assassinate me like they did President Kennedy, I'll serve two full terms. I'll retire with the fat pension and two hot Amazon bodyguards, one who looks like Shakira and shakes her pretty booty; and the other, perfect and refined, might pass for Halle Berry, and I will dress her up and show her at the opera and when I'm sixty-five I'll retire to Crete, become a Chinese American Georgia O'Keeffe and paint giant vaginas for the rest of my life.

I have no use for male flesh. I don't like men. I am a latent homo, no doubt. The dudes just don't look delicious to me. They offend my olfactory senses: dirty socks, stale beer . . . and when they're really sweaty they reek like putrid chicken soup. They make me gag.

I don't really like women either. They reek of soap and baby powder. They're always shopping and preening, like Mei Ling, aka Aphrodite bitch goddess, with her secret tattoo near her labia. You wouldn't guess that she has a high IQ, got perfect scores on her SATs, was declared a genius in fourth grade based on the way she chased after boys—like a delirious hussy.

VI.
SANCHO PANZA, or JUST WARHOL
MY VAGINA, WON'T YA?

Our last mission of the night is to deliver yet another party tray to Romero Electronics: they love pork ribs and orange chicken. But, oh no, Donny Romero, the firstborn, is Mei Ling's ex-boyfriend.

He once worked for our restaurant as a waiter. They used to spe-
lunk in the caverns of the soy sauce pantry next to the giant tubs
of fermenting tofu. Now he's on the East Coast studying art at
Yale. How spoiled is that? First-generation immigrant, and he gets
to study art. They've been corresponding: sending X-rated emails
and naked pics of themselves.

"Sister, do I need to tie you up?" I say. "Perhaps I better do this
a solo delivery."

She says, "Oh, I haven't seen Donny face-to-face since I got
my braces off. He has not seen me totally beautiful."

I say, "Strap yourself with the seat belt and don't get out of
the van. Just smile and wave and show your new teeth."

"How about I roll down the window and he can peck me a
kiss?"

"Okay, but you promise to not get out of the car!"

. . .

I carry party platter No. 16 down to Mr. Romero's office. Papa
Romero himself comes out: he's a nice jolly fellow. Too much
beer and chips gave him a big waistline, but you can see where
Donny gets his good looks. And being a big geeky child himself,
he always has something up his sleeve. He says, "Merry Christmas, young lady!" Out of the dark he pulls a giant yellow donkey piñata. Every year he gives us a big papier-mâché beast with
delicious treats inside: gumballs, candy, whoopee cushions, fake
poop, singing burro CDs, funny masks and stuff.

I say, "Gee thanks, Papa Romero, we always love receiving
your piñatas." He says, "Merry Xmas, Sancho Moonie, take care
of your Mei Ling Quijote Juanita." I think, damn, everyone's gone
literarily nuts?

. . .

I carry the yellow donkey to the van, where Mei Ling Quijote Juanita, strapped to the front seat, is French-kissing Donny. The entire front half of his body's in the car while his ass is sticking out, his baggy low-hung jeans showing his Calvin Kleins . . . so with all my might I give him a giant wedgie, and he squeals like a piggy.

"Get out of my way, pervert!"

He says, "So, Moonie, have you grown some titties yet?"

I say, "Shut up, Mr. Donny Romero Warhol. Go home and paint ten thousand copies of my beautiful vagina and post it on the Internet, won't ya?" I pull down my jeans to flash him my smiley butt cheeks. He and my sister have been puffing on a joint.

He says, "So, when you become the first woman president of the United States, you're going to crown me marijuana czar?"

I say, "Yeah, puff on, asshole, your brain will become peanut butter. Your mommy will have to wheel you around in a stroller."

His mommy is his soft spot. He doesn't like me telling tales with Mommy Romero in them.

I get into the car. He has a fast lizard tongue. I don't want to spend the rest of Christmas Eve jiving and jabbing with him. So what if he got to Yale, and he was captain of the debate team in high school. He's still a pothead!

Suddenly, Mei Ling says she's dizzy from too much Samoan punch. "Too much Donny pot," I say. "Too much face-sucking in one night will also do you in. You're useless. I should drive your damn ass home with this piñata, but I need your company. These are mean, boring streets on Christmas Eve. The camels are doing midnight Mass again."

VII.

SMOKED SALMON EGGNOG, or SHAKE YOUR CREDIT CARD THANG!!

Then Mei Ling discovers that she's left the credit card imprint thang at the Unitarian church. I am so pissed that I smash a handful of shrimp fried rice into her face.

She stuffs the rice into her mouth and spits it back at me.

"Oh, forget it," she says. "We'll go back tomorrow."

"No way," I say. "Granny will kill us. I don't want to have to drive this stupid van around after I'm dead."

So we return to the Unitarian church, and hippie-dude Jesus comes out again.

"Hey! Now pastor wants to invite you two in for dessert," he says.

"No, we can't come in," I say. "Mei Ling is sick."

"She looks mighty fine to me. Mighty fiiiine."

"Yeah," giggles Mei Ling. "I'm fiiiiine, as the dude says."

"You better control your pussy, sister," I say.

"I'll control my pussy," says Mei Ling, "only after I get some eggnog. It's Christmas Eve, and I deserve some eggnog."

• • •

It's impolite, I guess, to say no to the last left-wing church in southern California. So we walk into the belly of this weird eight-sided building. There is a beautiful, long table decorated with giant bows and ribbons and little silver doilies. The Chinese appetizers are mixed with a big turkey with red and green stuffing and a whole smoked salmon displayed on a glittery platter. Half of the people in the church are gay couples. The rest are your usual California rainbow-colored shake and bake, a democratic nightmare!

Everybody's pimped up in their ethnic costumes and designer gear. It's really a cool scene.

The pastor's wife gives us both eggnog. "No, thank you," I say. "I'm driving." So lusty Mei Ling drinks my share too. Then the gay choir starts singing "Silent Night." So poignant, so perfect. Little Mei Ling blots her eyes with a tissue. I want to gag. The guest choir, a motley hundred-member pimply crew from East San Diego High, sings "Hark! The Herald Angels Sing," sampling some fun moments of "Rudolph the Red-Nosed Reindeer," interrupted by a fat dude with a big scar on his face rapping over the choir, "Better not shout, better not cry . . . he's reading the list and checking it twice . . . Santa Jesus is a coming to town." He is funnier than shit. He's a freaky baby Marxist, but nobody dares to laugh. The whole church vibrates!

Mei Ling says, "I can see angels and hear stars. I close my eyes and imagine eternal love, world peace, all that good stuff."

"NOT! NOT! Who are you kidding, sister?" I shake her five times and slap her six to break her from the trance of facile enlightenment. They've been selling the church to us for centuries. "Remember the gunboats outside of Hong Kong? Remember how in one generation, Auntie Wu's family lost their minds, became Bible-thumping born-again Christians, and traded a Ming vase for a splinter of the cross? We're not going there, sister!"

VIII.
THE NEW MASTER OF THE FLYING GUILLOTINE
FLIP-FLOPS, or THE THINGS WE CARRY

"Yeah, I know that these people are progressive and well meaning. But let's be real. It doesn't matter if you're Democratic or

Republican, straight or gay. The rich whites will leave here and become richer, and the dark people will go home and work three shifts and plead for overtime. When the KKK gets wind of this place, they'll burn the whole church down! The revolution is not over, sister!" I raise my fist in protest.

And drunken Mei Ling says, "Remember the Zen saying: We must cast out false spirituality like a pair of old shoes!" She then leaps up, kicks off her shoes—a pair of three-inch platform flip-flops—into the air. One hits an innocent bystander—*bam*—on the head and decapitates his toupee. The other boomerangs *flip flip flip* against the wall and falls into a giant crystal bowl of eggnog. I have no choice but to shout, "Amen," leap out of the pew, sling Mei Ling over my right shoulder like a hundred-pound sack of Calrose rice and run like a wild banshee toward the parking lot.

IX.
PLEASE, JESUS, SAVE MY SISTER!

We get to the parking lot and I'm so winded I can barely see. Jesus hippie-dude comes after us. "Hey, give me a ride back to the college area."

"We can't," I say. "We have to get back to the Samoan 'hood with this Kahlua pig before our psycho granny flays us. Can't one of your loving, earnest peeps give you a lift on love? How about the bald one dressed like Joseph or the fat one dressed like the Magi?" I give him the stink-eye. I'm not going out of my way for anybody, not for Buddha, not for Jesus.

Out of the blue, Mei Ling says, "Moonie, I think that he should deflower you tonight." I say, "I ain't getting deflowered. I'm keeping the lid on until after medical school."

"Why are you so weird?" says Mei Ling. Then she turns to the lord and says, "You have to save my sister, Jesus baby. She's a virgin."

"A virgin at twenty? That's really weird. That's sick. Maybe that's evil. Certainly that's not healthy," says Jesus.

"What do you know about health, baby Jesus? You were a virgin birth, remember? You came out of your mama's vagina leaving her hymen still intact," I say.

"Maybe you're just asexual," says Jesus.

"I'm not asexual. Perhaps, I'm latent homo," I say.

"Latent? You're either homo or you're not!"

"So, Jesus. You know all about being homo, 'cause you've been jamming with the twelve apostles."

Mei Ling starts laughing like a hyena. Her face is bright red with white blotches all over because her liver can't break down the alcohol. It's the Wong curse. Nobody in our family can drink. I know that any minute now, she's going to barf and faint. I am still pissed-purple from having to rescue the drunken damsel from her flying-shoe episode.

"Shut up, bitch," I say. "Not everybody's a horny slut like you. Shit, if we all behave like you, there will have to be an abortion clinic and the line of protesters on every corner." I've had it with her and give her a swift donkey kick but miss.

Mei Ling crouches down in a horsy stance and tries to fake a flurry of eagle claw jabs, making Bruce Lee cat noises. With a serpent sweep, I kick her legs from under her and wrestle her down. She's drunk and wobbling, so sparring with her is easy. And Jesus—"Johnny," he insists now that we call him by name—is keen on saving my soul and popping my hymen for Christmas. He looks at me, drooling at the chops.

"Do you want me to keep the crown on or take it off?" Johnny says. Starting from his dirty sandals, peeling off his baggy jeans, he strips naked. The fucker doesn't wear underwear! Then the drunken savior falls flat on his back and blacks out.

X.
IS IT POSSIBLE TO RAPE A MAN?
AND OTHER ONTOLOGICAL QUESTIONS . . .

"Hey," Mei Ling says. "We have a naked dude in front of us. Let's take advantage of him!"

"No, we're women. Women don't rape men."

"Who says? And besides, it's not possible to rape men. Rape is a hostile act. We're not hostile, just horny and blessed with good imaginations. He won't mind. Actually, he would love it. Two hot Chinese girls doing him."

"But he's out like a sparkler. He's burnt wire, and we don't have his permission to violate him."

"Why don't you electrify him? I will give you a first lesson."

His penis is pink as a piglet. Why any pretty pussy would want to be entered by that is beyond me. He also has thick blond down from his throat all the way to his groin. A nimbus encircles his nuts. I have never seen so much hair in my life.

"We should do him a favor and give him a full body wax for his Christmas present," I say. I lick a clean hairless patch on his chest. He smells like sweaty jesus chicken soup; I start to gag.

"Lick him there," Mei Ling says. Even though his three-ounce brain is poached, his cock stands right up like a pink soldier with a funny helmet head.

"How can he be aroused while he's asleep? He must be pretending," I say.

"I'd sit on his face," says Mei Ling, "but I'm on my period."

"Disgusting," I say. "You were riding the Samoan dude's shoulder while you're on your period." It's getting really late, and the phone keeps vibrating with Granny's messages.

"How about we hide him in the pantry of the restaurant, behind the soy sauce cabinet?" Mei Ling says. "And talk sex with him tomorrow?"

"Are you kidding? Granny will have his hide. She'll flay him and hang him up with his brothers, the castrati pigs."

We decide to carry hippie Jesus back to the church because we don't know his home address. So we lay him down on his side like one of those divine odalisques in a museum, but on the front steps near a giant terracotta crucifix. Mei Ling wraps her hapi coat around him. Being way too small for him, the coat doesn't hide his beautiful jewels from the moonbeams.

Suddenly, I feel a rush of hot tingling from my pussy, and it slithers up through my Athenian pectoral muscles to my heart and straight into my throat.

I say, "Oh, no! I think I'm having a conversion experience. I'm a believer. I'm in love. I think I'm going to marry him and have two children, a cocker spaniel and budgies. I will have to postpone graduate school and end up teaching high school for a while until the kids grow up. Meanwhile, Jesus will get a shitty tech job and work inside a cubicle at IBM for the rest of his life. My immigrant dream has turned into a suburban nightmare!"

"Oh, oh," says Mei Ling, "out goes the White House, in flows the outhouse. You're on a slippery slope, sister." We finally stop and I say, "NOT NOT NOT! No chance, not in this immigrant American dream! Ain't no dumb-ass hippie Jesus dude in it." We both start laughing deep in our guts, *ha ha ha ha!*

XI.
THE RED VAN'S PENETRATING DOMELIGHT

There are twelve messages from our psycho granny, probably cursing us, calling us every animal on the lower rungs of the food chain—spittlebug, pismires, silverfish gonads! Mei Ling is snoozing in the back of the van in an embrace with the undelivered Kahlua pig.

I finally reach the Samoan Hawaiian Cultural Center. I drive up as quietly as I can, ring the door bell and leave the tray on the back porch. I can see through the window that the beautiful jock has his arms around a fatty blonde girl.

"Chinese food for supper, jelly for dessert," I yell. I drive off like Evel Knievel. I don't want the dude to give me a headlock for being an hour late and for biting him.

I am steering home. Mei Ling is still snoring, but I do not take the exit to the restaurant. Instead I make a U-turn and head east, toward the desert, afraid to face Granny's wrath. If she called us twelve times about the Kahlua pig, the Samoan aunties must have called her twenty-four times inquiring about it. And who knows how many mean-spirited, blue-haired church ladies reported on the flying guillotine flip-flops! So I'd rather drive east, toward the Sodom Gomorrah desert. I am not ready to face the cleaver. Not yet.

XII.
MOVE OVER NADIA COMĂNECI

I drive past an empty baseball field, and I can't help but stop: I have the itch to do two backward flips, followed by a round-off and a front somersault punch and land in Romanian-style Chinese splits. Mei Ling opens her drunken eyes to cheer me on. "Ten, ten," she cries. The flips are good, but I slip on the landing. "Eight and a half," Mei Ling shouts. "Points off for falling on your ass. Nobody's here to judge us but ourselves, so let's be judge, jury and executioner and cheat. Ten, ten, ten," Mei Ling yells.

I continue with two sets of drunken monkey tai chi a la Jackie Chan, combining northern tai chi with Granny's own machinations. "Roll on the ground like a hairy infant—drooping fists catch gnats—swinging tail on a baobao tree—stealing bananas through a cage—picking fleas off a sleeping cousin—stealthy kicks off a high branch." First, Granny invented the routine to make us laugh. Then she perfected it to become a full-body exercise routine, calling it "the dance of the mooncake vixen." My body and soul yearn for this discipline three days a week. It's in blood and muscle memory now. I close my eyes and I assume the form. It's as natural to me as breathing.

First Mei Ling and I do the routine in unison, perfect harmony. She's on the left and I'm on the right. We continue with some gentle sticky-hands sparring. Mei Ling's still drunk and wobbly, and I can feel her concentration veering off. She gets bored and starts throwing gumballs and jelly beans at a bunch of crows pecking on a roadkill. "Deathstars, deathstars, deathstars!" she yells.

XIII.
OH LORD, THE DEMOCRATIC VISTAS!

Mei Ling pukes up her guts onto an unsuspecting bird of paradise. I continue with a tiger-crane routine that Granny taught me when I was eight. The exercises make me feel energized, so

I get back into the van, eager to drive east some more. Mei Ling and I take turns shouting our grand ambitions for the rest of the night: *Let's go to Joshua Tree and spar with the cactus! Does that sound fun? Let's do double sword with the solar windmills! Let's rescue hunky tanned damsels and blond surfer dudes! Let's slay dragons! Let's steal from the Republicans and give to the poor! Let's drive south until we get to Baja. No, let's drive east and touch Arizona! Let's steal Patsy and Ratsy's father's Caterpillar and dig a hole to China! No, let's dig to Russia. I want to buy a Dr. Chicago mink hat. That's Dr. Zhivago, stupid! Let's eat at the all-night buffet at Viejas, throw it up and eat again. No! Let's do Barona—it's only 5.95 for all-night Italian. Let's catch a rattlesnake, give it to Granny so that she can drain its fangs and make medicine. Let's catch some scorpions, stir-fry them with ginger and onions and serve them up as exotic desert crabs! We'll make a million dollars! Let's stop at Agua Caliente and get a mineral bath and a Brazilian wax! Yes, an aloe facial and a Shiatsu massage too! Let's go to the Wild Animal Park and free all the animals in that cheesy man-made Serengeti. Let's turn on all the sprinklers and flood Torrey Pines golf course and ruin the Christmas Open for Tiger Woods. Yeah, we're tired of his perfect white-girl-loving, arrogant ass already! Let's order three short stacks at Denny's, eat them up and tell the waitress that we only ordered two. No, let's order five. I'm starving!*

Anything can happen tonight! I shove in "Silent Night" in Spanish, a CD fresh from the belly of the Romero donkey. I look over and Mei Ling is asleep again, snoring a girly-girl snore, whistling through her nostrils like a little bird. "Wake up, wake up!" I shake her. But she can't, or won't.

So I keep driving. I'm not going to worry about the destination. It's the not-getting-there. That's the real enchilada, I try to convince myself.

XIV.
DON'T YOU KNOW . . .

That every immigrant's tale is a comic romance? Once upon a time, a couple of absolute nobody girls named Wong are born. They load up a crappy donkey-van with bad Chinese food and drive in circles for ten hours. They smooch a few silly boys on the way (well, one of them smooches while the other beats them up). Then it never fails—by the end of the tale, those certain Wong-named-nobodies finally blossom into somebodies.

Or, do they?

Southern California mornings are always a fresh shock to the system, the black sky turning purple, turning blue blue, the empty freeway morphing into a river of honking vehicles. I nod asleep for a moment; then, without warning . . .

The sun slams through the dirty windshield and blinds me.

3

A Portrait of My Sister Sexing Tofu

Now the works of the flesh are evident: sexual immorality, impurity, sensuality, idolatry, sorcery, enmity, strife, jealousy, fits of anger, rivalries, dissensions, divisions, envy, drunkenness, orgies and things like these. I warn you, as I warned you before, that those who do such things will not inherit the kingdom of God....

—*Galatians 5:19–21*

Immigrant Dreams I

I dreamt that I came to this beautiful lush kingdom and all the boys were naked and had emerald eyes and sapphire nipples and ruby belly buttons. Their penises were long silver-and-purple-striped snakes with diamond eyes and flickering pink tongues. When I went up to them—to greet the boys—they would wrap their snake penises around my legs and arms and lick me all over with friendly greeting. I would pet their snakes without fear. I was having a very contented and intensely feely mealy moment with one blond-maned lad when my sister, Mei Ling, bounced into my dream from a high and messy willow tree. Of course, I was expecting her to appear to interrupt my happiness, always jealous as she is of my happiness, always with her secret desire to ruin my life with her petty neuroses.

Mei Ling was in a very foul mood. She was completely naked except for a red polka-dotted loin cloth that she suddenly tore off to reveal her nasty kitty. Literally, her vagina wore the face of a roaring pink kitty cat. Her kitty cat had yellow eyes, the proverbial single vertical slits dividing the pupils. She had a pink nose, long zigzaggy whiskers and hundreds of sharp, brass nail teeth. Mei Ling, true to her bratty show-off self, immediately wanted to conjure the great prowess of her kitty by squatting down on the riverbed to show me how her fabulous kitty could catch fish. Shit, I have never seen a fish-catching kitty before, much less one attached to my sister's vagina. So I said, go ahead, show-off, show me your fish-catching pussy. Mei Ling squatted down. Her kitty gurgled and snapped and in seconds caught a little silver minnow. The poor little minnow didn't know what struck him and started seething about in the kitty's mouth. The kitty swallowed the minnow tail first, and when it finally came to the head, she bit it off at the neck with her sharp teeth. After a few minnows, she went for bigger game: trout, sea bass. Then she went for two nasty-looking barracudas and finally one gray toothless shark. (That shark, I think, was an algae-eating kind.) You could hear her crunch down on the shark's cartilage and make loud gulps as she urged the large beast down her throat, unhinging her little mouth way back to make that final snap to bite off the head. Each fish she would swallow tail first and bite off the head in the last gulp. (Obviously Mei Ling's kitty did not like heads.) The river was filled with floating heads: minnow heads, trout heads, barracuda heads, salmon heads, bass, and one big, angry-looking shark head. Their myriad eyes gleamed in the sun.

Mei Ling stood there laughing loudly, her arms akimbo, her kitty meowing and hissing, roaring and guffawing with her. I was very perturbed at her arrogance and pomposity. Who does she think she is? Barging into my lovely dream with her nasty fabulous kitty. Of course, I looked down at my own vagina. I didn't possess such a fine animal. How common it was. My vagina had a small tuff of black fur and that was all. My pink labia were soft and toothless.

Then one of the blond boys, whose snake I was petting, turned to Mei Ling and attempted to wrap his snake around her thigh. Before I could warn him or push him away, the kitty, who was singing and mewling happily, let out a loud roar and grabbed at the snake's head. The snake shrank fast enough to get away. Then it coiled and lunged back, hinging its head back to reveal two huge tonsils before it grabbed the kitty's face in its mouth. The snake became rapacious then, and greedy. Not only did it desire to swallow the kitty, it designed to swallow all of Mei Ling, vagina first. Helpless without her fierce kitty, Mei Ling started screaming. I was laughing of course. Serves you right, Ms. Kitty vagina, Ms. Fish-eating show-off roaring pussy!

By then the snake had already swallowed Mei Ling up to the waist. Mei Ling was now really screaming and crying and calling out my name. The snake, which was so beautiful, turned into a huge ugly serpent. The serpent hissed through gooey slobber and my sister's blood steaming out of its nose. Fireballs caromed out of its eyes. Suddenly, there, I had to rid myself of all jealousy and animosity against my sister and try to save her. She was, after all, a beloved member of my family.

I immediately emptied out my big black purse to find a weapon. Fuck, I had not cleaned out my purse in a year, filled as it was with hairballs and shit. I felt around in it. I kept finding coins from Taiwan. Those with that ugly Chiang Kai-shek on them. Damn, I never converted my money from my last trip to Auntie's. You know, I must change my evil ways and start to get organized. I could never find anything in my apartment or my purse, the hopeless black cavern. How will I make anything of myself?

I finally found a nail clipper from last week at Target, a 2.50 purchase. How did I know that it cost 2.50? Well, Mei Ling bought one for 1.75 the week before, and I was miffed that she got it on sale and cheaper. Well, I took out my silver nail clipper and started clipping away at the serpent, pinching little holey wounds all around its neck. It had my sister as a mouthful—it couldn't attack me.

Losing all control over his serpent-penis, the boy started crying and screaming and swinging at me. But he missed me every time. I was very short for my age and ducking and swiftness came with that territory. Meanwhile, yellow goo leaked from the little wounds that I made with my nail clippers. "Stop, stop eating my sister," I said, "or else your penis will leak yellow goo for ten thousand years." But the clipper wounds were too wimpy to make the serpent stop. Just when I thought it was the end of Mei Ling, our cleaver-wielding grandmother suddenly appeared in the dream.

She wasted no time. She assumed the form of an eight-armed bodhisattva and whacked off the ugly serpent with her trusty cleaver in one hand. With another she whipped all of us with her bamboo feather duster. We started screaming and crying for our lives. With her third hand, she pulled Mei Ling out chamber after chamber from the serpent while with her fourth hand, she gathered all the fish heads so that she could make fish head curry for supper. It was a secret recipe she got from one of her Indonesian Chinese mahjong buddies. With her fifth hand, she was already chopping a giant onion. "This will enhance the pungency of the fish heads," she said. With the sixth, she wiped her brow. With the seventh, she dialed her cell phone to call the boy's mother. "Bad boy mother," she said. "Come take bad boy home. He no welcome to my house no more." She continued whipping all of us with that bamboo duster. Mei Ling, bad boy with chopped-off serpent, and me—all snot-nosed and crying. With her eighth hand, she gestured a conciliatory mudra toward heaven.

After bad boy's mother arrived and took bad boy away, Granny made me and Mei Ling sit in the corner with two teapots on our heads. The teapots were filled with high mountain green tea. We had to sit in the corner balancing those teapots with warm streams of tears coursing down our cheeks. We would balance those teapots on our heads for hours, days, months, deep into our adulthood. We both cried and cried. We were very, very sorry.

Immigrant Dreams II

WADING

We are both wading in the brilliant blue Pacific. Two pretty Chinese sisters. You are floating on your back and staring into the sun, the sun blinding you, and all you can see is the reverse of sun, which is a red corona against shimmering blackness. But this doesn't bother you. You are fearless. You don't even need to wear shades. You are wearing a pink polka-dotted bikini, vintage Sandra Dee, 1955. I am floating face down, looking at the pretty fishes. You say I'm always the one looking at the pretty fishes, stupid optimist of a breech birth that I am. I'm wearing a day-glow white polyester one piece, vintage Elizabeth Taylor in *Suddenly, Last Summer*, 1959. We're both into that virgin/whore look. Because I am a bad swimmer, I am buoyed up by two large arm floats with rubber duck-heads on them.

Once in a while, I come up for air and contemplate the two coast guards in the distance floating in their patrol boat. One is fat and swarthy and gross, scratching his groin. The other is thin, buff, gorgeous, with long blond locks and smoking. They both are staring out into the blue horizon. Bored and listless bastards, they're supposed to be looking for drug smugglers or Mexicans. Or they're just here to pose as Bush's bogus orange-alert poster boys. As if Bin Laden's going to waste his time bombing the OC and kill a bunch of money-grubbing yuppies, immigrants and beach nobodies. I say, I'll take the skinny one. I can reach up and unbuckle his belt and pull down his bell bottoms, give him a blow job, and as he throws his head back in ecstasy, give him a quick wing-chun jab to the throat and drown him. Meanwhile, you take the fat one, reach up, give him a blow job. You don't like giving blow jobs, but do it anyway—it's for our freedom—and as he is struggling with his pants, you karate-chop his nose and drown him. Then we can steal the boat and veer it toward the promised land.

You ponder this for a moment. "Why must I have the fat one? I always get the fat one. Granny always gave me the fat, misshapen dumpling nobody else wants. It looks like a lump of shit, and you always get the pretty skinny dumpling, with the corners pinched perfectly upward."

I say, "Do you want to cross the border or not? I say it's not about the body. It's about the boat. It's not about the blow job but escape. It's not about choices at the supermarket, but the freedom to make those choices."

You say, "Yes, but it's about self-respect. I can't always have the shit dumpling."

"All right," I say, "I'll take the fat one. I'll unbuckle his gargantuan belt. I'll drag him with all my strength, pull him down. I'll give him a blow job, and when he's perfectly into it, I'll drown him."

And then you say, "Hey, wait a minute. You're tricking me. Isn't big always better? Bigger fries, bigger burger, bigger Cokes? Isn't that the American way? Aren't you using reverse psychology on me to make me think that I would want the skinny one when actually there is more to love in the fat one? I am not going to give you the satisfaction. I'll take the fat one, after all."

I say, okay, whatever. Meanwhile, in the heat of our ridiculous altercation, the men and the patrol boat—*poof*—disappear!

No fat one, no skinny one. We missed the moment, sister. We missed the boat. We spent too much time lollygagging: Emersonian freedom or Jeffersonian democracy. Two fat ones, three skinny ones. Three chimps, four humpbacks, five orangutans. Who gives a fuck? Your high-minded speeches about justice got us nowhere. The boat is gone. We will never get to the other side. We will never reach paradise.

Immigrant Dreams III

A PORTRAIT OF MY

SISTER SEXING TOFU

My sister, Mei Ling, is murmuring in her eight-legged bliss, lying betwixt and between five 200-pound bags of Calrose short-grain rice and a giant tub of fermenting tofu. She is an eight-legged creature, not because she is spawn of the phylum Arthropoda but because she has the blond surfer dude on top of her.

From this vantage point, cock and cunt are linked in a staccato rhythmic carapace—whose appendages are four hairless, four hairy, four thinner, four thicker, four brown, four white, two parochial-school white anklets and patent leather shoes, two white crew sox and dirty white Nikes. They are groaning, thumping, slamming, cooing, laughing, having great sex.

Save for my Hello Kitty undies, I am naked and am hiding behind a hanging shower curtain with daisies on it. I have my contacts out and am wearing my black-framed spectacles, peering through my brand new palm-size teeny-weeny Sony spy-cam.

One cannot say that this creature loves, can one? It is ultimately headless, heartless. Mouth seals mouth, genital seals genital. Eyes closed, it cannot discern the world around itself. It cannot feel danger. It is totally self-absorbed, insistent upon satisfying its basest needs. And one knows that it is not conceptualizing anything deep—not the latest on string theory or conjugating Latin verbs or unraveling an awkward Homi Bhabha sentence: *"If, for a while, the ruse of desire is calculable for the uses of discipline soon the repetition of guilt, justification, pseudo-scientific theories, superstition, spurious authorities and classifications can be seen as the desperate effort to 'normalize' formally the disturbance of a discourse of splitting that violates the rational, enlightened claims of its enunciatory modality."*

No need to wonder why Mei Ling prefers to be united with this inferior creature. The surfer dude is not alpha material. He's matriculated into the pipe-fitting associate program at the community college. He has been working at our family restaurant for two years now—as a busboy—trying to graduate to kitchen help, but he cannot peel onions without crying. And never mind the long line to the status of "waiter," where the real money is made. No, he's no alpha male, not even a beta. He's the flea on the dog's scrotum. But wouldn't you know it, he is endowed with a big—no, huge—no, colossal—no, mammoth—no, gargantuan—no, mega-gargantuan schlong! Nobody dares to argue with perfection.

I am crouched next to a giant cask of rice wine and my eyepiece is getting fogged up. I am of the order Vicarious Voyeurous, my sister's arch nemesis. For no reason at all, I might yell, point and rat on her just for spite. In the small communist country of Wong, sisterhood exists only as a cheap surveillance system. We are steadfast to our Marxist-Hegelian principles. We take the idea of social equality seriously. No one strays from the nest without the other following. A hemp rope is tied to our sisterly ankles so that one does not stop and tarry around the melilotus and munch on jungle berries while the other goes home to the gulag and does the chores. Today, it took me six hours to quarter 254 free-range chickens, disinfect the bloody butcher blocks with Lysol and, on my hands and knees, scrub down the filthy grout with bleach and a toothbrush.

Somehow, without tutelage from the tribe, Mei Ling understands pleasure for its own sake. She is not looking to procreate with this backward lad, for getting serious with him would mean dragging her down, pinning that beautiful copulatory ass to the small town of Piss River, Oregon. Alas, we might as well seal her up in a jar of formaldehyde.

Mei Ling is obviously satisfying an itch, which is unheard of in immigrant behavioral history. One must not satisfy one's itch. One must sit up straight, cross one's legs, keep one's focus on one's homework and forge onward toward one's future. Mei Ling has three more months of ghastly parochial school, but we're not Catholic. We are forced to go to Catholic school because our Buddhist grandmother thinks that the nuns will give us discipline. Phooey, ha ha! Thank goodness that both of us will have an escape valve and will be going to university on a full scholarship in the fall.

If you scratch an itch, that itch could turn into a wound. That wound could become infected, and then that infection could spread, becoming gangrenous, and bloom beyond loss of just a limb or two. It might infect the abdomen, curdle the brain and leech into the soul. It could ultimately mean the death of your tribe and your people. Exercising self-control does not mean merely exercising your vulva-sphincter muscles. Or orchestrating orgasms. Self-control means self-abnegation, means shelving the hormones and the libido, postponement of sex, courting rituals and even bowling until after law school or medical school. In short, one must not disappoint the elders. One must sew up one's gonopore pussy for the common good.

Suddenly, the left patent leather shoe drops to the ground. In an ear-shattering sound, the vinegar and soy sauce bottles tremble on the shelves. A minor coitus-interruptus and the creature rolls over once so that the surfer dude can be bottom.

I am watching with stoic bemusement and wondering should I or should I not call Granny down to see this spectacle. This would definitely be a number ten on the Richter scale of Mei Ling spectacles. Scale one? The Mei Ling sex-cam caught the amusing but benign incident of the vixen French-kissing Marcus Marcus. Can you believe this? His mother gave him his last name as his first name. It's tautological. And talk about the lack of tribal imagination! Scale two, the cam recorded a perfect wide-angle shot of her kissing both Marcus Marcus and hand-jobbing Julio and Coolio all at once. There was no penetration involved, so I've labeled the flash drive "blackmail" and stashed it in a vault for a rainy day. Scale three, she was blowing off Marcus Marcus while peeling potatoes with a paring knife. The act was so fast that the evidence fizzled into the drain of the disposal.

One must bring down the libidinous prima donna with a great fall. She's a fat operatic dirigible that one must shoot down with a bazooka. The creature must be exposed. She had always worn that slutty thong under her prudent parochial uniform. She has long danced on that edge of high peril singing, *Nah, Nah, Nah!*

She is the master of deception. By day, she's a straight A student. By night, she's doing it, in full defiance, in the Great Matriarch's food cellar, doing it to the hilt in the alcove of plenty. Let's get a slow, close-up dolly shot of the giant tubs of fermenting tofu. In one tub labeled *"Don't touch! For Vegan Wedding"* four hundred squares of veggie flesh jiggle. They sit quite emphatically between five casks of rice wine imported directly from Shanghai and twenty-seven jars of marinated kohlrabi (the Matriarch's special delicacy), skeins of fresh green onion and giant wintermelons—roots and marl and all—pulled from an organic Chinese veggie farm in Fresno, gallons of peanut oil in shimmering tins, troughs and troughs of soy sauce, vials upon vials of fragrant sesame oil. All throbbing ovulae and sperm reservoirs.

She/I—the dreamer—cannot act as a principal in her own dream. She, the narrator of the tale, is an easy accomplice. She sits quietly on the sidelines at the dance, waiting to be invited. The watcher has a bitter place in the world. She has so much yearning in her heart, so little acumen. Her loneliness is unbearable. Her unrequited longing calcified into her ventricles. Her silence welling up in her throat, all she can do now is gasp or sing for blood. She must quench her thirst for revenge. She must sound the sirens. She must rage out for being the obedient one, for being the repressed singer, for being that perfect Chinese girlchild too timorous to break the mold.

· · ·

So the creature of deception, camouflaged, carapaced, inches across the dark room, grunting, hissing, brandishing ecstasy. Any second, the female will open her mouth and tear off his head. I have seen Mei Ling tear off the heads of many an innocent marauder: turbaned, baseballed, Rasta-dreadlocked, doo-ragged, ponytailed, spit-shine bald. She is a collector of heads. Beheading a man during coitus could provoke tintinnabulations of joy, so says the Kama Sutra of orb weavers.

I hear the Great Matriarch walking down the stairs. She is adorned in her black cloth kung fu Mary Janes. She has walked in these ugly shoes for eighty years. She treaded them from the jade steps of the Forbidden Palace to witness the horrific rape of Nanjing; from the dark, dank Yenan caves to the Great March, then straight through the Buddha-slashing, red-flag-waving folly of the Cultural Revolution. I hear her coming, wind in the sails of a ghost ship. Not *boom, boom* or *click clack*—but *swish, swish, slide, slide*.

For a cold moment I feel all powerful. I am the guardian of the peaceable kingdom and I could change fate. Shall I be benevolent or cruel? With whom shall I align myself? What are my selfish motivations? I have been waiting to expose my slutty chameleon sister. I have been jealous of her perfect breasts and slutty attitude under those parochial school uniforms. Perfect grades, perfect SATs. I have been waiting to force her to her knees.

But why should I align myself with my cleaver-wielding grandmother? She's a Confucian tyrant watching over our virginity. A reverse racist—trying to keep our blood pure and untainted by barbarians. She is controlling and repressed. She could not give her girls freedom because she herself has never been in touch with her sexual self, has never loved another. She has never known beautiful abandon. She was a picture bride to my ailing grandfather thirty years her senior. She gave in only because she ran out of revolutionary movements to join, and she had promised her mother at her deathbed to marry. She was a nursemaid soon after she became a bride. And for years, she has pushed our hard-working parents aside to reign as self-appointed keeper over our libidos.

To do nothing, according to Lao Tzu, is an activist's assertion. To do nothing, according to Martin Luther King, is a ticket to our own destruction. Moral apathy hides less than good intentions.

I am slip-sliding into moral decay. A lazy long-spined character with bad thoughts and bad intentions will certainly spawn bad actions. I will burn in Buddhist hell. Yama will pluck my liver out and boil it and eat it with ginger.

So with both hands across my mouth, I close my eyes tight and do nothing. I let the Great Matriarch descend into the pantry to find what awaits there.

She is swishing and singing and carrying her cleaver. She is mumbling to herself. She will go to the pantry to cut a piece of a giant wintermelon for Mr. Goldstein. Mr. Goldstein must have his wintermelon soup, sprinkled with dried shrimp and scallions. The giant wintermelons are thick-rinded tuns of flesh and are the size of fat infants. She is swishing, humming an old Sung Dynasty magpie tune. No, instead of going to the wintermelon bin situated in the opposite corner from the creature, she takes a sharp turn toward the giant vat of tofu and bends down to scoop out two squares with the flat of the blade. "Must make mock duck dish for table three," she mumbles.

This is where the dream turns into nightmare. I, the observer/ dreamer, naked save for my Hello Kitty undies, hiding behind a plastic shower curtain, behind the dishonorable spy-cam, shall record my grandmother as she exacts my sister's fate. In one mighty strike she lowers her cleaver and chops off an arm, a hairy one, one with a wristwatch. But no blood gushes. The wound heals itself immediately and a brand new, even hairier arm grows back with brilliant red fur. This infuriates the Great Matriarch, so she chops another, a leg, a smooth tanned leg, with a white knee-high and black patent leather shoe. She chops and chops, but it is curiously obstinate and refuses to break off. Finally, the leg tears off at the knee-bone like a slim door falling off its hinges. Then another fresh leg grows back: hairless, tanned, shoeless, sockless, smooth as a baby's leg. She chops and chops, one breaks off, a new one emerges. She severs limbs; new limbs immediately appear. She keeps head-bent, cursing, chopping. Alas, the Great Matriarch's work is never finished.

Suddenly, I regret that I did not warn Mei Ling. Out of self-ishness, out of moral cowardice, I let the Great Matriarch begin this bloodless carnage, locked in this eternal hell of offense and defense, lopping off, pinching back, only to trigger a fresh bud to surge forth. How tired my grandmother must be lowering the cleaver over and over. How tired my sister creature—who only wanted some nasty rebellious fun, but is now caught in this eternal nightmare. How tired the surfer dude, rapacious fool, caught in an intergenerational power struggle, for which there is no reprieve— between ancestral law and this vestigial sister vessel. This mind-less beauty, a hothouse flower caught in the blade of the eternal bifurcated argument, between obedience and freedom, love and tyranny, repression and bliss, devastation and rebirth.

I am still standing behind a plastic curtain, naked save my Hello Kitty undies, paralyzed with guilt, yet trembling with fear. I have recorded the evidence. I shall edit it, label it, vault it for history, but what does it prove? That ultimately life is bloodier than food storage? That art imitates bean curd, and that even bean curd cannot transcend its own essence and deny itself of the pri-mordial jiggle? I utter a prayer for quick atonement: *Amaduofu, amaduofu, amaduofu.*

Mei Ling stands up, smoothes down her parochial plaid skirt, matriculates Harvard.

Duets

Y ou speak English very well, Mrs. Wong. I am most impressed.

—Thank you for your kindness, Mrs. Jones, but, no, actually, my English is quite wretched.

—No, I am not patronizing you at all, Mrs. Wong. Really, you speak English very well, especially for a foreigner. Oh, I suppose that's not the way to put it. We are all foreigners in this God-awful Colonial outpost. Nobody is indigenous here. Are we?

—No, no offense taken, Mrs. Jones. My people came from Guangzhou after the Communist takeover in '49. We're all strangers here. No, my English is quite substandard. I learned it in the orphanage in Hong Kong from an Italian nun named Sister Theresa. She had a thick Sicilian accent but purported that she spoke "the King's English" and not "the Queen's." So my English is quite wretched really, but I guess it's tolerable for a Chinese housewife in Hong Kong. Most of my people refuse to even bother.

—No, really, you mustn't dismiss yourself that way. Haven't you read *The Second Sex*? We women must stick together. I heard from Mei Ling that you were widowed very young. You raised such fine daughters all by yourself. You are truly an accomplished woman. Let's put all false modesty aside, shall we? After all, my Douglas wants to marry your Mei Ling. We're almost related already. Our bloods, almost mingled.

—Yes, I read *The Second Sex* in a very bad translation from French into Italian, finally translated into vulgar Chinese by yet another unsavory Italian nun named Fenolossa.

—Well, my dear, you deserve an A+ for your fine unsavory Italian English. Why, my husband and I have been living in Hong Kong for thirty years and we don't know a word of Chinese. We've become so used to impeccable translators hired by his firm to cater to us. I dare say that I can't even go to the corner store to get milk. I have to point and make comical gestures in shape of a cow to make myself understood. The storekeeper stared at me humorlessly and must have thought, "What a total moron this woman is." Oh, what a delicious banquet you have made for me. You shouldn't have spent so much of your valuable time in preparation. I am sorry that my husband and Douglas are in the States this moment and won't be able to enjoy these divine goodies with me.

—Oh, again, Madame, you are being overly generous. The table is quite modest. I hope that we have not offended you by its paucity. Just morsels for my esteemed American guest.

— But I learned from your daughter that you have been cooking since Tuesday. That's four days of grueling preparation.

— No, you are mistaken. I think daughter No. 1 meant to say Thursday—that I've been preparing since Thursday, which was yesterday. She gets her days in English mixed up. She's not a very good student. I must admonish her constantly so that she will be more diligent. "You must get your days of the week right," I tell her. "What happens if you miss an appointment? What if they say to come Tuesday to collect your one thousand pounds of Sterling and you appear Thursday and the money is all gone?" But she's a stubborn, lazy parasite and will not listen to me.

—Oh, the fish is so tender. The flesh just kisses off the bones. I am amazed how you people know how to cook fish so perfectly.

—Oh, you are being generous again and flattering. I am sorry that this grouper is such a small fry, hardly a teenage fish. Not a grown-up, we should have sent it back to the fishmonger. He's a fast-tongued crook. I should have had a harsh word with him and his band of half-wit cormorants. Most fishermen use trawlers these days. I should tell him, bloody trawlers!

—Your daughter, Mei Ling, is very beautiful, and I am thrilled and proud that she will soon be a part of our family.

— No, again, you've mistaken, my dear Madame. She's a very plain, ordinary creature, my No. 2. Look at her, sitting there as sallow as a turnip. Her lips tight as a purse.

—No, I beg to differ. Your Mei Ling has perfect porcelain skin, which is only one of many reasons why my Douglas is very attracted to her.

—No, my No. 2 is too dark, like a peasant. She likes to play in the sun instead of going to Pipa lessons on Fridays. My uncle espied her on Lantau Island, sunning on a big rock, licking a custard popsicle like a lizard, when she should have been taking lessons. I am afraid that she has ruined her perfect porcelain skin.

—Furthermore, your daughter has a fine disposition, very quiet and polite. This is another reason why my Douglas is so attracted to her. Chinese girls are much better behaved than American girls. Douglas says that Mei Ling never says a bad word

95

about anybody. She always keeps her negative opinions to herself. She is always very considerate of the other person.

—No, Madame, you must not flatter us with such kind words. Mei Ling does not have a good character. She is stubborn, willful and she does not appreciate our tutelage. You just don't know her. Her quietness, her politeness is effrontery. She is quiet because she is secretly gathering information about her victims, so that she can release evidence against them during a later argument. She is not harmless. Look at her, with eyes darting left and right, entertaining evil thoughts. I don't know why your Douglas wants to marry her. She has a questionable moral character. She is an impudent little vixen.

—You know, it's not good parenting to criticize your daughter like that. Especially not right in front of her. In the States, we call this "child abuse." You know that children could sue their parents for verbal abuse, for hurting their self-esteem and fragile egos. I saw a show on *60 Minutes* about this. You should be very careful.

—Yes, you are very compassionate to be so concerned, but really, we don't tolerate substandard behavior from our children, especially from No. 2, who was raised by her devout Buddhist grandmother. Above all she should understand virtue. Born with the temperament of Kuan Yin, she was the most merciful child. But now, she has turned into a manipulating little hussy. I am afraid that if we don't punish her regularly, there will be no turning back.

—Oh dear, I think we should change subjects. I dare say that if your intentions are to repel us away from marrying your beautiful daughter, your attempts at subterfuge are of no consequence. Douglas has made up his mind. And my husband and I are both completely taken by Mei Ling's beauty and grace. Nothing you can say or do can interrupt the wedding plans now. By the way, the stuffed black mushrooms are quite exceptional, so pungent in that rich oyster sauce. I taste a tinge of seaweed and five spice. You must give me your recipe so that I can give it to my cook.

—No, again, you are too polite. The mushrooms should be bigger. They should be the size of Buddha's fist, not the size of his thumbnail. They should be steamed a little longer. The stems are just too sinewy. And No. 1 forgot to go to the market to get more ginger. We need thin slivers of ginger to tease out the mushroom fragrance. I must sever her allowance right away. She has been daydreaming about boys instead of concentrating on her tasks.

—Now, I must protest. As a mother myself, I know that children do make mistakes. According to Dr. Spock, we must encourage children to make mistakes. Too much perfection makes an unhappy, anal-retentive child. In fact, I must protest very loudly. I am very concerned about this. I strongly oppose your severing your child's allowance because of a few missing shavings of ginger.

—Not shavings, my dear Madame, I said slivers. Which are a little larger and longer than shavings. No. 1 is a science prodigy. She is a recipient of Her Majesty's Royal Scholarship. She can distinguish between two shavings of ginger and two slivers of ginger. Two fingers of ginger as opposed to two knuckles of ginger. An iota and not a smidgen. A tad and not a pinch. After all, she is matriculating Oxford in the Department of Applied Mathematics. She practices the art of precise measuring.

—Goodness, the temperature is getting very hot in here. I must lie down for a moment and wait for my driver to come back and take me home.

—I am sorry, Madame, the air-conditioning is very poor in Hong Kong. The machines are not as powerful as the types that you get in the States. I told my No. 1 to buy the South African brand. But she's a political agitator, just like her Boxer grand-uncle, and she refused to buy anything politically questionable. Apparently, the lot of South African air conditioners available in Hong Kong was purchased from the apartheid government in the eighties. No, she just couldn't bear it. So she bought a cheap Aus-tralian brand instead. What are Australians anyway—not British, not American? Not Japanese. They're situated so far south that their brains are in their bums. I must admonish my No. 1, the would-be scientist/engineer. I am afraid that she didn't properly adjust the digital controls. She must have been dreaming about Hollywood again. Every engineer wants to be Spielberg. But I say to her, in this house, you first must tend to earthly chores. A bad air conditioner is not a virtual reality. And do try a piece of the salt-baked squab. They're fresh from the New Territories. A squab on the skewer is greater than a rooster in the hand, or something like that. Do make yourself at home and eat more. I'll ask No. 2 to make you an iced chrysanthemum tea. She has a special healing recipe. One drink will cleanse your soul. Some sweets perhaps. Egg custards from the "floating bakery." No. 1 bicycled all the way to Repulse Bay to retrieve them for you. They're so smooth and rich, they'll slide off your tongue. I see that you're turning a bit pale and clammy. Don't fret—No. 2 will wipe your face with a cool washcloth soaked in green tea. She has miracle hands—"Buddha's citron hands"—she can give you a heavenly neck rub. Don't fight it. Do, do lie down. I am not afraid of "the takeover," are you? We Cantonese are very sturdy. You know the Confucian couplet, "Kingdoms come, kingdoms go, but the family is forever." Then, of course, you westerners say, "If you can't take the heat, get out of the kitchen." Or something like that. I still have problems with idiomatic phrases, thanks to those unsavory nuns. Look, look to the west, beyond Repulse Bay. Can you see the black clouds gathering up into a violent storm? The monsoon will soon purify the heavy air. You'll see, Hong Kong will be fragrant and beautiful next week. You know what they say—in the Colonies, it's not so much the heat as it is the humility.

Reductio ad Absurdum

I t is a mistake to believe that a distance composed of an infinite number of finite parts must itself be infinite.

If we keep dividing a mooncake from ½ to ¾ to ⅛ to a fraction of that, and a fraction more, will we finally eat nothing?

So Mei Ling is trying to walk from her disheveled bed to the doors of the restaurant called Double Happiness; she keeps walking.

Now she is halfway to the door, now halfway of the halfway, now half of that. Will she ever reach the door, will she ever come out to the other side of freedom?

Consider the property itself: Mei Ling's bedroom is in the back of the house. The giant kitchen occupies the middle distance between her disheveled bed and the restaurant's front doors. The Lotus Room, an ornate pink womb reserved for private parties, fills the middle distance between the kitchen and the front doors. The middle distance between the Lotus Room and the front doors contains the hostess desk where Mei Ling and Moonie spent over ten years of their lives, five days a week, taking reservations and escorting customers to the inner sanctum.

Some might say that you can try to leave the restaurant, but the restaurant will never leave you. The soy sauce and garlic have forever stained your hair. The blood of ten thousand sacrificed animals has seeped into your soul. Oh, how can you leave your village—mother, father, sister, cousins, grandmother? How can you leave the angry, silent cook, the singing waitress and the cutie busboys? How can you leave Mei Ling and Moonie to their indiscretions?

Meanwhile, Mei Ling is taking off her satin red hapi coat, then the soy sauce–stained white blouse under the hapi coat. She takes off her embroidered cloth Mary Janes, pulls off her black skirt and nylon stockings. Pulls up her hip-hugging Levi's and black T-shirt. Shrugs on her black leather jacket. She is doing all this—pulling off, pulling on—while she is inching toward the doors, the doors that say "Double Happiness" on them.

And while inching forward, she takes out her compact mirror and puts on some lip gloss and opens up a tube of liquid eyeliner, stops for a silent moment and paints on perfect lines on her eyelids with two graceful strokes.

She will never leave the restaurant called Double Happiness. Yet, she shall always be leaving the restaurant called Double Happiness. One must not stay too long at the restaurant called Double Happiness. It has always been a transient state. It has always been a waiting station. The immigrants must have new dreams for their children.

The parents worked twenty-hour days so that Mei Ling could escape the restaurant called Double Happiness. They put her through Harvard so that she could have a new chance in the first world, so that she won't be sentenced to a life of drudgery, so that she won't have to work in a sweaty kitchen at the restaurant called Double Happiness. The second generation must have bigger dreams: they must become doctors, lawyers, scientists, real estate tycoons, computer-geek geniuses. They must not linger in the restaurant called Double Happiness.

Yet, they shall never escape the blood red womb of the restaurant: those ornate walls and faux lanterns; kitchy Sung paintings of gaffer-hatted fishermen and hanging cliffs; tigers and fair ladies, pagodas and pandas, dragons and phoenixes, rocks and birds and dainty, gilded flowers. A garish *chinoiserie*, a mock imperial kingdom that no longer exists . . . or perhaps, never existed.

Now, the grandmother is wondering: Who is Mei Ling meeting up with? Could it be Donny Jesus Romero, driving his father's Lexus to take her to the movies? Could it be Baby Yang of the great Yangs, driving up in Father Yang's Benz? Will he take her to the computer fair?

Where is Mei Ling escaping to? What paradise awaits her on the other side? Whose engine is idling? The grandmother ponders this as she peeks from behind the curtains. Her lips purse into a deep frown. Alas, what is waiting for Mei Ling is a souped-up, beat-up Camaro driven by the surfer dude.

When one leaves one predicament, does one necessarily arrive at a better place? When one leaves an embattled homeland, will the shores of exile be safe haven? When the supermarket contrives too many choices, will we find the sweetest melon? Who is this slacker prince who refuses to dream, who is himself the end of a long prosperous rainbow? Why does she love him so? There is no money in his pocket. No poetry in his soul. No brilliance in his vision. Why can't she see what her grandmother sees? A dynasty that has long been defeated by drink and laziness. Wantonness and stupidity have addled the brain of a great nation.

From inside his souped-up Camaro, he opens the door for her. The motor is running, his left hand still on the steering wheel. Incense and faux-leopard seats, hard rock blaring. The arm that has opened the door for her many times is tanned with a blond down. She loves this arm. She loves touching the tattoo of the gleaming sword on the forearm, three drops of crimson blood painted at the sharp tip near the sinewy wrist, and the inner arm: Oh, merciful Buddha, the blade is trellised by a tender ribbon of roses.

Moonie's Penis

Patsy and Ratsy, twin sisters (speaking in unison): This is a true story—one day after gymnastics class, Moonie said, "Wanna see my penis?"

We all know that she's a baby dike. She always wore Dickies overalls and a Yankee baseball cap backward. And during diving or gymnastics training, she would get a buzz cut. She's not cute either, like her sister, Mei Ling. She always has a mean look on her face, like, don't bother me, I'll bite ya! So right there in the locker room, she pulled off her leotard and her panties and there it was: a little bouncy penis. It was pink and smooth and uncircumcised like our little cousin's from Montpellier. (We saw it once when we had to babysit him last summer.)

Then, she started dancing and pirouetting on the tiles. *"I have a penis. I have a penis, na na na."* She was bouncing and bouncing. Her little pink penis was bouncing up and down with her. Then she stopped spinning and said, "Wanna touch it?" We were so shocked that we didn't know what to do! So we both screamed and ran home and told our mother.

Our mother called Sissy Goldman's mother and Sissy Goldman's mother called Priscilla Whiteman's mother and Priscilla

Whiteman's mother called our assistant gymnastics coach, Mrs. Blanchard. They all went down to Vice Principal Ramirez's office yelling, "We can't have freaks on the gymnastics team!" But the vice principal refused to do anything and called us "identical, congenital liars!"

Then our mother took it upon herself to call Mrs. Wong. Mrs. Wong thought that she was a crank caller and said, "No penis, we no serve penis," and hung up the phone. Finally, our mother told the Churchlady, and the Churchlady said, "This must be the devil's work. Those heathens, they worship idols and grew a penis." So the Churchlady bullied the Pastor into going to the Double Happiness restaurant to pay the Wongs a visit. And a bunch of us went along for the spectacle. When we got there, Mei Ling was the only one around and guided us to the Lotus Room, where Moonie was folding napkins and doing her chores.

The Churchlady ordered Moonie to take off her clothes. She didn't object and took off her hapi coat and her black skirt and panties, and she uncovered her little pussy with no fur on it. Then both Mei Ling and Moonie started laughing and singing, *Meow meow meow*. And Moonie, to show off that she's the star of the gymnastics team and that she's better than us white girls, did three back flips and a round-off, landed in the splits and continued her mocking cat dance, singing, *I have a little pussy meow meow meow.*

The Churchlady gasped and covered her mouth. The Pastor said, "Oh Lord," and covered his eyes. Our very own mother turned bright red and covered her ears.

4

After Enlightenment, There Is Yam Gruel

(THIRTEEN BUDDHIST TALES)

After Enlightenment,
There Is Yam Gruel

When Buddha woke up hungry the animals offered him their favorite food. The baby sea lion offered him day-old fish bits that her mother regurgitated. The jackal offered a piece of smelly rotting meat infested with maggots. The squirrel monkey offered a handful of bruised bananas, veiled with gnats. The hare was the most selfless of all. She went into the forest and gathered an armload of wood, lit it on fire and placed herself in the center as sacrifice. Grandma Wong, exhausted from long hours at the restaurant, was not impressed with the feast. She handed Buddha a broom and said, "Old man, sweep the back porch first, then the filthy hallway," and went to the kitchen and heated up last night's yam gruel.

Why Men Are Dogs

A long, long time ago in Hong Kong, a man and his dog died side by side, both asphyxiated in a hotel fire. The Goddess of Mercy, who happened to be jogging by with her pedometer, decided to bring them back to life. She examined the man's body and saw that his heart was shriveled and diseased by smoking and bad eating habits, but the dog's heart was still in good shape and was red, plump and healthy. She discarded the man's diseased heart and replaced it with the dog's heart. For the dog, she made a beautiful vegetarian heart with soy paste and wheat gluten. She said some mumbo-jumbo New Age prayer and the dog sprang up and wagged his tail and barked in gratitude. The man, instead of thanking the Goddess, growled, scratched his balls and tried to bite her head off for manifesting too late and for not serving him steak tartar for dinner and not saving him from the British Empire in the first place.

That Ancient Parable about Nanzen's Doll

Moonie and Mei Ling were fighting over a Barbie doll. *The church ladies gave it to me!* said Mei Ling. *No, they gave it to me!* said Moonie. Grandmother Wong grabbed the doll by its platinum ponytail, pulled out her big cleaver and hacked it straight down the middle. *Here*, she said, *the lamb and the host*, and went back to the stove and sautéed some day-old turnip dumplings.

Gutei's Finger, Redux

Gutei cut off his student's finger, put it in a bowl of chili, sued the restaurant, got two million in a settlement, divided the booty, fifty-fifty, with his freaked-out pot-head student and called it *satori*. Twenty years later, on his deathbed in Macau, flanked by beautiful tanned boys, he issued his last email to the world: *The finger, the finger. I give you the finger. Ha ha ha ha!*

Putai

There was a homeless man who ran around Wanchai shouldering a burlap knapsack. He called himself the Happy Buddha and told everybody to call him "Putai." My grandmother said, "He's an imposter. I know Putai when I see Putai and he's not Putai." Nevertheless, he made a very good impression. His knapsack was bulging with toys and candy, and he gave them out to all the undocumented street orphans and refugee children. Then he ran around and opened his filthy hand toward the passing businessmen and said, "Give me a dollar." Because he was such a benevolent presence, almost everybody would pull out a dollar from their wallets. But my grandmother was not a believer. One day, with me and Mei Ling in tow, she followed him onto the Star ferry to Kowloon and trailed him from the Golden Mile all the way to Mong Kok, shouting, "Fool, charlatan, you are not the manifestation of Buddha!" He tried to escape her, but she followed closer, almost stepping on his heels. He walked faster, laughing, taunting her, chanting, "Putai, Putai, Putai."

One day, we saw him lying on his back on a bench. He stayed motionless for several hours. Mei Ling ran up to him saying, "Putai, Putai, where's my candy?" but he didn't get up. Later, our neighbor told us that some gangsters had lodged two bullets into Putai's eyes. They had come to collect their debt. Apparently, he had been betting on horses with his cumulated dollars and had finally lost the big one.

Thereafter, for many years of our childhood, every time we walked by that bench, Grandmother would point to a stain and say, "Herein lies the proof. He was not Putai."

Ryokan's Moon

Mei Ling was sitting at the campsite, waiting for her boy-friend to come back from the 7-Eleven. A creepy junkie, stoned out of his mind, came trembling toward her. He said, "Take off your clothes, bitch!" She said, "No way, I'd just bought this faux Dolce&Gabbana denim camping outfit from Hong Kong, and it took me two months to find a seamstress to alter it. Go take somebody else's clothes. That lady three trailers down, she buys only couture." The creep looked dazed by her response and left.

Ten minutes later, the creep came back, still so stoned that he could barely stand up. "Bitch, take off your clothes," he said. She said, "Okay, obviously, you came a long way to do this." So she took off her clothes and gave them to him. "Okay, now, go away and sell them on eBay. My dead grandmother would be blissed out in Nirvana that I give them to you. You know, the right inten-tion, the right action, all that Buddhist crap. And here, take my money. All I have in my wallet is twenty-three dollars. I gave my boyfriend the rest of my cash to buy beer and nachos. By the way, he's coming back soon, so you better get going." The creep looked bewildered and took the clothes and went away.

Twenty minutes later, the creep came back again. "Shut up, bitch, I'm going to rape you. And don't try to fancy talk me out of it either." Mei Ling sighed but was still cool. "My grandmother, the Buddhist, would want me to be compassionate and give you what you want. But she would also want me to tell you the truth. I cannot speak falsehood. Yama, the king of Hell, will boil my tongue in oil if I do. The truth is that I have a hideous infestation of the crabs. I caught them from my ex-boyfriend the punk rocker. (Notice, he's an ex-boyfriend now. My new boyfriend is okay with my checkered history. He was raised by feminists.) I bought some medicine from TJ that turned my pubes blue. This stuff is so harsh that it might make your dick fall off." Indeed, he looked at her pubic hair and her little stubbles, leftovers from her last Brazilian wax, were scintillating bright blue. He groaned in disgust and went away.

Meanwhile, Mei Ling sat naked and stared at the beautiful full moon. Ryokan would have given the creep the moon. But she was not that enlightened. Not yet. She wanted this magical moon all to herself. It was a warm and fragrant twilight, and the wild jasmine had just opened.

The Equanimity
of All Things

The Great Matriarch says to Mei Ling, "I'll give you three bananas in the morning and two in the evening." Then she says to Moonie, "I'll give you two bananas in the morning and three in the evening."

Moonie sulks for half a day, unhappy with her lot, and says, "Granny, you must treat us equally; we're in America now. We're no longer in colonized Hong Kong or feudal China. We must abolish the class system. There must be equal justice for all."

So the Great Matriarch says, "All right, I'll give you three bananas in the morning and two in the evening." And Moonie walks away satisfied, believing that she has set things right for herself and for others in the same predicament.

Later, when the Great Matriarch revisits this episode to tutor young girls, she refers to this lesson as "the deceptive equanimity of all things."

Third Eye

When Grandma Wong first held up her new granddaughters Moonie and Mei Ling at the hospital, she noticed that they both had a large golden birthmark in the middle of their forehead like Buddha's third eye. As the babies grew older, the birthmark grew larger, and a crimson orb-of-a-mole emerged on the center like an all-knowing eyeball. Mrs. Wong was a non-believer, generally, and not superstitious. Although she claimed herself to be a good Buddhist, in practice she was an agnostic materialist and saved half of her money in an emerging market mutual fund and half under her mattress and paid for incense at the temple only after a sharp downturn in the market or to fend off an imminent tsunami.

Auntie Wu urged Grandma Wong to take the girls to see the Dalai Lama next time he came to visit Hong Kong. After all, he was the CEO of all Buddhists. He should have an enlightened explanation about this birthmark. Or, at least, he could give her a ballpark number as to what the girls were worth. Remember, just last year, the little girl Sajani was plucked from the streets of Nepal and was elevated to "Living Goddess"! Perhaps the twins are the latest manifestations of the Buddha. Grandma Wong heeded Auntie Wu's words and made an appointment with the Lama's secretary almost nine months in advance of his visit; and came the day, she hired an expensive hovercraft taxi to get to the temple on the island of Lantau. When she got to the front desk, a stone-faced nun handed her a number, then directed her to a large waiting room.

Upon entering the waiting room, she was disappointed to see that it was filled with hundreds of proud and blissful grandmothers with their special girlings in tow. They all had shiny red birthmarks on the center of their foreheads.

Impermanence

When Grandmother Wong gave Moonie and Mei Ling their one-month-old haircutting party, she invited her old cronies from the village. Auntie Lu said, "Look at Mei Ling's long fingers. She is going to be an accomplished violinist like Sarah Chang and Midori!" Auntie Lan said, "Look at Moonie's alert eyes, flashing left to right, already weighing evidence. She is going to be a fine counselor of law. She will be the Johnnie Cochran of Hong Kong!" Auntie Wu said, "How sad—we humans and our delusions. The only certainty about any baby girl's future is that she will die. She is already a soon-to-be-dead person."

To this remark, Grandmother Wong grabbed Auntie Wu by the ear, dragged her out the door and kicked the door shut.

Wiping One's Ass
with the Sutras

The Great Matriarch caught Moonie using a page from the Buddhist Sutras to wipe her ass. Moonie says, "Grandma, between my duties in the restaurant and my studies, I have been too busy to go to Wal-Mart to purchase toilet paper. And all I have within reach is the study manual for the MEdCATs and an old copy of the Buddhist Sutras that Auntie Wu sent us. So, which do you prefer—that I tear a page off an important study guide, one which may contain crucial information that may make or break the prospect of my becoming a brain surgeon in the future; or that I tear a page off the Sutras, which is written in ancient Chinese, which I can't read anyway?"

To this, the Great Matriarch issues a long sigh and says, "Pull up your underpants, girling, they're dragging on the floor."

The Theory of the One Hand

he girlchild thrusts out her left hand.

The Great Matriarch says: *What if I cut it off, skewer it and sear it over briquettes for a Mongolian barbeque?*

The girlchild says: *Okay, Granny, weird, whatever you say.*

The Great Matriarch says: *What if I flay it like salmon sashimi, into fine thin pieces, display it on a large celadon plate with orange rind garnishes and feed it to your half-wit sister?*

The girlchild says: *Okay, Granny, gross, whatever!*

The Great Matriarch says: *What if I dice it with my scrap-iron cleaver and mix it up with ginger and scallions into a clear miso broth to feed the world's orphans?*

The girlchild says: *Okay, Granny, tee-hee, then that would be a benevolent, useful hand, wouldn't it?*

The Great Matriarch says: *What if I grind it in a meat grinder, mixed with the ears of your illegitimate Japanese forefather, the entrails of your surfer-dude boyfriend, the clavicle of your Mexican ex-husband, the pancreas of your half-black hip-hop fuck-buddy in the afternoon and the tonsils of your half-green hippie fuck-buddy in the evening?*

The girlchild says: *Granny, stop spying on me! They're not fuck-buddies. They're just friends; well, friends with benefits . . . Tee hee. Okay, Granny, then let's call it "California Cuisine."*

The Great Matriach says: *I am not joking, girlchild.*

The girlchild says: *But it's all very funny.*

The Great Matriarch says: *No, it is not.*

How Was I Conceived?

How was I conceived?" questioned Mei Ling. Grandma Wong answered, "When you were yet unreborn, and still in the process of reincarnation, your mother came home from a long day at the electronics factory and had a severe earache. Auntie Wu used a pair of magic bamboo tweezers and removed the worm from her ear. The worm was as teeny and wrinkly as a monkey's penis. Auntie Wu placed the worm in a gourd and covered it with a jade plate. In two days, the worm transformed into a funny-looking spotted dog that had a scratchy bark that sounded like *Mei Ling Mei Ling*. So we named her 'Mei Ling.'

"I know that this story sounds very strange to you. But all family stories are strange. You'll get used to that."

Lantau

While sitting prostrate before the ivory feet of the great Buddha, I spilled almost an entire can of Diet Coke on the floor. I quickly tried to mop up the mess with my long hair. I peeked over my left shoulder: the short nun said nothing and averted her eyes. To my right, the skinny old monk was consumed by a frightful irritation of his own. He was at once swatting and dodging two bombarding hornets that were fascinated by his newly shaved head. "I hope he's not allergic," I giggled. And beyond us was the motherless Asian sea, glittering with the promise of eternity.

5

Beasts of Burden

(SEVEN FABLES)

Once upon a time, a hawk caught a quail with violence and swooped her off to his high nest to be eaten. While in his sharp talons, the quail said, "I shall forgive you for this action, sir. I am to blame for my own misfortune; it was I who foraged on unlawful ground, in a foreign region not of my ancestors. . . ."

—*From a Buddhist fable*

Liars

My name is Epimenides Wong. And I declare that all Chinese girls are liars. I am, clearly, a Chinese girl; therefore, I am, without a doubt, a liar!

I am also half Cretin. It's all my mother's fault, I'm afraid. Yep, she did it with the rice merchant. But that's another dirty ditty, which I won't go into here, lest I get sued for defaming the character of a desperate people, one that is even more tyrannized and demoralized than my own. Not to mention, I would bring shame to my mother's memory. She had long discarded her whoring days for a saintly seat next to the Great Buddha. Did you know that we had to pay three thousand American dollars to a shaman-adept to cleanse her reincarnating organs? And it's ancient knowledge already that Cretins, too, are liars. It has been proven (and I am the living proof) that they are both motherfuckers and liars! Alas, I am a liar all around, irrespective of the fact that I am also a half-breed Chinese Cretin bastard.

Don't believe anything that I say. Perhaps I am not a Chinese girl at all. And if you call me a Cretin, I'll slap you. And good God, you know the truth, only in your worst Freudian Oedipal nightmare would your mother lower herself to fuck a Cretin.

Generally, mothers are sexless creatures who patrol around the house wearing ratty slippers. Nobody would want to fuck them, not even the rice merchant. And I don't know which is the more gruesome image: your mother wearing a dowdy ketchup-stained floral house dress and ratty slippers, or my mother wearing a dowdy soy sauce–stained floral house dress and ratty slippers.

If truth be told, I did not spring from the loins of the family Wong at all. I suspect that I was sired by wolves and was weaned by the family Canidae. And they too are notorious liars. Look at them: mangy, shifty-eyed, foul-smelling, lying here, there, all over the imperial outposts, around dying fires, telling tawdry tales, chortling at the moon.

The Wolf and the
Chinese Pug

One day the wolf, the last survivor of his pack, was so hungry that he finally leaped over the barbwire fence and crossed the border into the suburb. He sniffed from house to house, toppling garbage cans for food until he focused on one large white house somewhat hidden from view behind two oddly shaped cypresses. He smelled animal presence and was delighted to find a small Chinese pug barking at him in the backyard.

He went straight to the pug and said, "Don't bark, comrade-sister, hear me out! Why are you with those pasty white owners anyway? They dress you up in a shabby brocade kilt, put a stupid coolie hat on you. They make you fetch their newspapers and dance on your hind legs. They get a big laugh out of you when their neighbors say, 'My, what an ugly face on that dog; it's so ugly it's cute.' In return for your party favors, all they give you is cheap dog food. Don't you have any self-respect? Haven't you heard of post-colonial self-reliance? It's the twenty-first century, baby! Take off your leash and collar, set yourself free! Gandhi freed his people. Mandela freed his people. We must not be occupied! We are cousins, you and I, we are of the same blood. Why don't you run with us, hunt with us, go wild! Don't you know, you are really a wolf in pug clothing? Domesticated creatures unite! We must start a canine revolution!"

Indeed, the pug had been unhappy, but she couldn't put her finger on the nature of her unhappiness. But then, again, by bourgeois habit we've personified the creature by presupposing that she can understand happiness in the first place. So let's say, she's been uneasy lately, a bit nervous. Dogs, if they can't discern unhappiness, perhaps are armed with a sixth sense and feel ominous forebodings: the onset of storms, the presence of dangerous beasts that might cause harm to themselves or to their owners. Presently, the appearance of this pushy wolf had increased her anxiety.

She had never seen a wolf before. Although this creature possessed four legs and a tail, he had bad breath and spoke in a gruff, unappealing manner. He had a huge nose and a long drippy tongue. Why should she trust him? He was not her kind. For every virtuous liberator, there dwells a heinous dictator who oppresses his own people: how about Kim Jong-il, or Saddam Hussein, Pol Pot, Idi Amin, Stalin, not to mention, the most dastardly of them all, Hitler? The list is endless. Then, with a nostalgic tear, she considered the Rochesters, her English owners. They picked her out from a litter in Hong Kong. They prided themselves their empathy, for choosing the smallest, most vulnerable one. Thank goodness; otherwise, she would have ended up roasted and served on a table at a fashionable Guangdong restaurant or dragged by the nape and drowned along with other unwanted doglings.

She wasn't so clear about her identity in the first place: What is a pug, anyway? Is a Chinese pug really Chinese? Whatever she had become was a result of thousands of years of evolution, inbreeding and serendipitous genetic engineering. And if one were not so clear about the reason for one's existence, why bite the hand that feeds one?

The pug said, "I'm sorry, Mr. Wolf, but no deal. Please go away, or else I shall have to bark loudly and alarm my owners." But as she turned away, the wolf leaped on her and bit her throat and proceeded to tear open her abdomen in a few ghastly chomps.

Then the wolf squeezed through the swinging dog door into the kitchen and saw Mrs. Rochester standing in her orange and pink appliqué floral apron. First, she was alarmed, but then, when she saw pieces of the pug's fur and blood in the wolf's teeth, she screeched, "What have you done to my little Mei Ling?" and raised a pan of hot sizzling bacon off the stove and showered it on the wolf's head. With the wolf howling in pain, she went into the bedroom and brought out a twelve-gauge shotgun and shot him five times in the face, not missing a single shot. It just so happened that she was trained as a marksman by the Scotland Yard in their elite antiterrorist forces.

· · ·

Obviously, there shall be no revolution tonight. The Rochesters will conduct a solemn ceremony and bury whatever is left of poor little Mei Ling in their backyard. The remains of the wolf will be dragged away and incinerated in a local blast furnace operated by the city's animal rescue unit. In a year or two, the Rochesters will go to Hong Kong and purchase another Chinese pug pup: the tiniest, most vulnerable one of the litter, of course. They are good tender-hearted Christians, after all. And, oh, how they love that breed of dog.

Fox Girl

There was a so-and-so Mr. Famous Poet, who had a bad reputation around the country for sexually harassing graduate students. The usual fare was that he would go on a college book tour, get stark raving drunk and chase dark, exotic-looking female students (yes, he preferred the exotic ones) and try to lure them to his hotel room. He was as well known for his gluttony and voracious appetite for gourmet food, drink and lechery as he was for his poetry, faux pastorals with shepherdesses and wooly sheep all over the green hillocks of Arcadia. Because he was so famous, nobody bothered to tell him that groping female graduate students was no longer cool. Nor in his acclaim did he realize that policies had been put in place in universities for such behavior. He could actually get fired. Likewise, nobody bothered to tell him that his poetry was no longer relevant. The great Norton Anthology in the sky had already replaced his entries with a younger, hipper Croatian Navajo surrealist.

One day, he was on the last leg of yet another reading tour. He landed on a Midwest airstrip near a famous writing program surrounded by bean and corn fields and majestic hog-feeding operations. A young graduate student on a research fellowship was assigned to drive Mr. Famous Poet around. She was to pick him up from the airport, take him around town to get his fill of peanuts and Bombay gin, deliver him to a local bistro for supper with other writers and graduate students. Finally, her last task of the evening was to deliver him in one piece, drunk or sober, to the university to give his poetry reading.

The graduate student was a little Chinese girl born in Hong Kong and raised in San Francisco, around five foot two, a bit thin but spunky, with a confident spring to her walk. Presently, she was writing a critique on Brecht's "Alienation Effects in Chinese Acting" and was finalizing an experimental poetry thesis filled with reverse fables, in which little girls speak in the personas of the most hapless and vilified of animals. With activist zeal, she wrote compassionately on behalf of the pea-brained stegosaurus, the doomed dodo and common roadkill. She mocked up an entire new vocabulary to sustain the wealth of sounds and utterances foreign to human ears.

Almost as soon as she introduced herself to Mr. Famous Poet at the airport, he grabbed her breasts and said, "Why don't you and I ditch the rest of them and go to my hotel room?" The student turned beet red in the face and said, "Okay, Mr. Famous Poet, whatever you say, but in exchange, you have to pull some strings and get me a tenured teaching job preferably in California." He said, "Of course, my influence is long and wide and reaches all the way to even California."

But as soon as they both entered the car, the girl started yelping and shaking as if she were possessed by a demon. Her long black hair volumed up into a fluffy red coat. She grew a perfect little perky pink snout and a huge, magnificent tail. Before his very eyes, she turned into a beautiful red fox. She quickly leapt onto his lap, rubbed against his chest and climbed up onto his shoulders and bit his ear with a seductive little growl. He was mesmerized by her. Her wild fur and musky perfume gave him an urgent hard-on. A violent rush of passion shot into his groin. He was so turned on that he could already feel the sperm percolating on the great bulb of his penis. He had never fucked a graduate student fox before. Never a wild animal—a few tame lambkins and his own cocker spaniel—but never a wild animal. So he said, "Hold on, hold on, little red fox," and went to the trunk to get condoms from his briefcase. One cannot know what kind of sexually transmitted diseases are harboring inside fox vaginas, he thought.

When he got back into his car with his ribbed Trojans, the fox suddenly transformed into another creature. Her beautiful red fur suddenly turned stark black. In one bold stroke, a brilliant white stripe raced down her back as if it were a dividing line on the highway. The fox on his lap had suddenly turned into a two-hundred-pound gargantuan skunk and before he could throw her off, she raised up her skirt-of-a-tail and sprayed a foul yellow varnish all over him.

• • •

This poet really stinks. I am not being so much literary but literal. He smells like he hasn't taken a bath for months. He professes that he is writing an epic, not just a personal epic of the likes of Whitman, which he deems as an inferior kind, but a classical epic of the likes of Homer, filled with gods and heroes in full regalia. Henceforth, he has no time for taking a shower and doing things that ordinary mortals do. He shall, for the rest of his life, traipse around his apartment wearing a tattered, terry-cloth robe, inhaling hand-rolled cigarettes and drinking endless goblets of Bombay gin spritzers. With such modest talent and penis size, he shall spend his last days wrestling the ghost of Homer.

. . .

The revelation of the poet's putrescence soars all the way up the hierarchical food chain. First the small magazines reject his poems. Then the poetry society rescinds its invitation. The Ford Foundation formally withdraws its fellowship money. His putrescence can't be masked by huge emblematic perfumy flowers or grandiose adjectival phrases.

Much sadness befalls this lecherous poet. He can no longer partake in groping young females because none could stand to be close to him. Nobody invites him to give readings because his epic is boring. The Pulitzer Prize shall elude him. The Nobel committee shall opt for a mesmerizing lyric poet from the sub-Saharan desert who writes in Swahili.

One fine day, as he is contemplating a poem and delighting in a jar of sweet pickles and as he is looking out his office window to the lawn, a beautiful little fox saunters by, her fluffy tail arches way up, like the headdress of a proud warrior. At first, he feels a small renaissance in his pants; then he is stricken with an overwhelming fear and repulsion, putting to flight the triggering aftertaste—weirdly sweet and bitter—of nostalgia.

Beast of Burden

P lease don't pity me. I know my fate. I was born a donkey and I must die a donkey. I am a beast of burden—my brown hide gashed a thousand times by the whip of my master. He is as brown as I and twice as angry. He is bitter and hardened for disease and starvation has killed two of his children. The tsunami took two more. None would live past infancy. He takes me to the mountains in the morning, and I haul a pile of wood back at night. Dead man's wood, illegal wood, they call it. It doesn't belong to us. It belongs to the crown princes and the corporations. The police have orders to shoot us on sight for poaching it. This doesn't stop the master from poaching. Poaching is his only means of keeping alive.

One day, the master went away to a distant village to attend his uncle's funeral. He forgot to latch the corral, and I decided to run away. I galloped for miles without looking back. I hated that paddock, that worthless land. I hated the master and his sour-faced wife. I wanted to flee, travel far away and never come back. Then I stopped at a stream to drink. I saw a tigress bathing under a waterfall. She had taken off her magnificent skin and left it spread out on the rocks. As I admired her beautiful skin from afar, I had a brilliant idea. I said to myself, I want to be top of the food chain for a day. I want to be honored, respected, feared and even loathed. I was so desperate that I would give anything to have that day, even my life. So I dared to walk up to inquire of her, "Ms. Tigress, if you let me wear your skin and be a tigress for a day, I will come back and offer my life to you. You can flay me, devour my flesh and use every part of me. I am so tired of being a beast of burden; I just want to have one day of paradise on earth."

She looked at me and laughed. "Look at you, stupid bitch-donkey, all skin and bones and you think that I would waste my breath. But because you didn't steal my skin while I was bathing and are so courageous as to approach me without trepidation, I shall honor your wish: you may borrow my skin for a day. However, you must return it to me by dusk tomorrow because I am going to America next week to become a new member in the endangered animal exhibit at the San Diego Zoo."

So I slipped on the skin and marched into the village. Upon seeing me, the people screamed with fear and ran into their houses. I was having a ball, running around, eating apples from the carts and ransacking millet from the granaries. I ate my fill then lay down under a large mandrake tree for a rest. Then a gang of men with crude weapons ran toward me and cornered me into a pen. One said, "Bastard tiger, we'll kill you first before you kill us." So they chased me around the pen, shouting, hitting me with their hoes and scythes. "Don't kill me," I cried, "I'm not really a tigress. I'm only a donkey." But they continued to come toward me, hitting and wounding. One shot from his old musket but missed.

Finally, I managed to escape and ran into an abandoned mine shaft and slept through the night. In the morning, I felt severe pain all over my body as if my bones were crushed. But, as promised,

I returned the skin to the tigress and limped home. My master saw me from a distance and said, "You idiot she-ass, trying to run away. I'll show you who is the boss!" So he whipped me hard for an hour. The wounds that the villagers made opened even wider. Finally, when I could stand no more, I collapsed onto the hard ground and closed my eyes to my beastly suffering.

The villagers carved up my body and ate every inch of me: my bones made soup; my flesh made stew; my hide they stretched into a giant drum and each night they beat the drum. Even in death I would not escape their beating. For leagues and leagues, through the ravaged ravines, between the clefts of typhoid mountains, into the tired and steeping jungle and beyond the malarial rivers, you could hear the drum beating, beating, beating the skin songs of a doomed people.

Cicada

The cicada is out of his shell. After seventeen years sub-merged in the dank earth, he is bright-eyed, horny and ready for action. He is trilling on a leafy bough, calling for a mate, but he stops to drink some droplets of dew off a waxy philoden-dron—so loving the dew that he doesn't hear the praying mantis lurking behind him. Intense in her focus, ready on her haunches, the praying mantis pounces, taking the cicada head first, crunch-ing and relishing, so she can't feel the swift-footed sparrow behind her. The sparrow twitter-twitters, light on the branch. She jabs her sharp beak and skewers the mantis, devouring her in three mouthfuls, so relishing this morsel that she doesn't sense the small calico cat with a spotty black nose, ready to pounce on her. So fun-loving is this calico, Beetlejuice, that she plays with the limp carcass in her mouth for a few minutes. She rolls the spar-row around on the ground with her paws. So focused in her play, she is oblivious to the California red tail hawk, high on her perch, poising herself, collecting the gravity to swoop down to snatch the poor, declawed kitty to feed her famished chicks.

The next day Jack, my asshole neighbor, keeps tripping around in his yard and, calling "kitty, kitty, kitty," finds only a bloody fur pelt on the ground. He points his rifle at the red tail hawk, shoots a few times and misses. He says, "I'll get you, bastard." I say, "Leave the poor bird alone, you loser-redneck, else I'll call the police. She's an endangered raptor." "You shut up, wetback bitch," he says. "Endangered raptor, my ass. The fucking bird ate my cat. You're lucky that I don't shoot the whole lot of you."

. . .

The next month his company sends Jack to Iraq to fix some sabotaged oil field pipes. He stops one day under an olive tree for a moment's rest and delights in a care package of Almond Joy candy bars that his mother sent him. So hungry is he that he can't eat just one but proceeds to unwrap another and another. As he is relishing each morsel of the fourth candy bar, a sniper from atop a building shoots him in the back of the head. The marksman jumps up and down waving his rifle and shouts, "God is great, God is great." So boastful and elated is he that he is not aware that the enemy is behind him. Scarcely has he cried out "God" a third time when he is strafed down by a UH-60A Blackhawk assault helicopter.

The pilot of the copter says, "Shazam! Got five in one!" Finally able to return home after sixteen months of combat for her reward, a brief R&R in Hemet, California, she finds that her loser-husband has run off with another woman, a lieutenant colonel, higher brass than hers. The house is emptied of furniture, save a moldy mattress. After throwing the mattress out the back-door, she sits on that mold-stinking perch, wearing her comfy Hello Kitty flannels, and downs a quart of Bombay gin with Led Zeppelin blaring into her headphones. So deep into her despair that she tunes out the ten thousand cicadas performing an eerie birth and death song. They sing and sing. They shall finally meet their mates, make desperate love and perish satiated. Or they shall be eaten by other famished creatures, and the cycle of feeding and mating and suffering begins again.

· · ·

The dead and the living shall bury themselves and be reborn over and over, with the same lust for life, the same fury. The egg-born, the womb-born, the moisture-born, those with form, those without form, those with consciousness, those without consciousness, those who are neither conscious nor unconscious: all singing together, in one loud hissing harmony.

Piglets

After their mother died, the piglets continued to suckle on her teats. The milk was still warm and tasty to them. But after a few hours, they noticed that she was stiff and cold. They nudged her with their noses, snorting and crying, trying to wake her. Finally, they no longer recognized that she was their mother and they scrambled away in fear. Except for one piglet who refused to depart. She lingered, snorting and crying, waiting for her mother to awaken.

Suns and moons came and went. Putrescence set in. A fetid stench pervaded the world. Kites and crows descended, disemboweling her, air-lifting her limbs, and ten thousand maggots, worms and cockroaches polished her bones. The piglet stayed, crying and squealing, still waiting for her mother to regain consciousness.

Why, Great Matriarch, shall there always be those who cannot recognize their mother when she is still whole and those who cannot detach even when she has been shattered? Why this eternal contradiction?

Meanwhile, the piglets went on with their piggy lives, carving territory, buying houses, trading up and down the margins of the stock market, losing all memory of their beginnings. Only that one piglet, crow-pecked and weakened by the vermin, kept steadfast by her mother's side and was never conquered. She couldn't keep a man and couldn't hold a job. She was arrested twice for vagrancy, hospitalized several times for hearing voices. She sometimes wrote a poem; she sometimes found a dress at the Salvation Army Thrift Store. A dress, a poem—such discoveries gave her temporary joy.

One day while she rummaged through a garbage can in the suburbs, a pretty housewife came out and chased her away. She immediately recognized that this woman was her sister and said, "Mei Ling, Mei Ling, remember, the six of us used to frolic in the woods? Remember uprooting delicious tubers in the jungle? Remember snuggling under our mother's belly in the cold? Remember the shade we shared beneath the very same belly in the heat?"

The woman answered, "I am sorry. I don't know you. My name is Heather Jones and I was born in Poughkeepsie to two important professors."

. . .

But storyteller, you may ask, why introduce this paltry character to us, what is the purpose? Tousle-haired, dirty-faced, alone in this vast universe, rooting through garbage and overturning stones: her life is failure.

. . .

She survives to remember.

Twin Birds

When Moonie was seven, she found a three-legged turtle in the backyard. She didn't know where it came from, but her granny said that all turtles are sacred and must be protected. So Moonie kept it in a large sandbox she made out of an old wooden tub where her granny used to ferment tofu. She fed it leftover veggies from the restaurant and dead bugs and worms. One day, Nasty Marcus took it from her and threw it down on the pavement, and tried to shatter its shell. "I want to kill it," he said, "but I can't. It's tucked up inside its shell, and the shell won't break." Moonie said, "I know how to kill it. Granny says that all we have to do is throw it in the water and it will drown." And Nasty Marcus said, "Okay." And they took the turtle down to the stream and the turtle swam away. Nasty Marcus was angry that Moonie fooled him and he tried to punch her a few times, but she ducked and avoided all the punches, except for one, which she deflected with a downward block. Then she kicked him in the shin and sprinted away. She stopped at the top of the hill, stuck out her tongue at him and yelled,

"Moron, loser, father-fucker!" and completed the insult by flipping him twin birds with both hands.

. . .

And Marcus would never forgive her for that last gesture, never.

6

Ten Views of the Flying Matriarch

Die before you die and you shall never die—

—Sufi saying

Ten Views of the Flying Matriarch

JESUS ROMERO, TOWN MAYOR

The Double Happiness restaurant used to be over there—you see that large house being renovated near the riverbank? After the old lady died, the girls sold it to the Pham family and now it's going to be a Vietnamese restaurant. In the beginning, the Wongs were quiet people. They didn't give us any trouble. Double Happiness was a thriving restaurant for fifteen years. The food was mediocre. You know, the eggrolls were soggy, the sweet and sour pork was bright red like candy, the fried rice was probably three days old. You know, the Chinese who come up here to the hodunks of the Pacific Northwest don't give us the "real" Chinese food, only the fast Chinese food they think we want. Well, they didn't give us any problems, except for a rat infestation once in a while, but all restaurants contend with that. Her two granddaughters were really pretty in their red satin hapi coats, and people in town made it a part of their life to eat Chinese food once a week. This is an old logging town, and people are poor. She kept her prices down and hired quite a few neighborhood teenagers to work in the kitchen and deliver take out. She was real conscientious that way. But then, there were stories of her kung fu hocus-pocus, that she was flying around, beating off boys who tried to hit on her granddaughters. I said, "Hogwash." You know, it's boring around here. People don't have much to do but gossip and make up tall tales. Until one day, the missus and I had company from Vancouver and we all went down to the Double Happiness. We ordered their best dishes: moogoogaipan, black bean spareribs, and the house special, soy sauce duck. We had a great evening, drinking and eating, and when we all went home, I realized that I had forgotten my wallet. I had just cashed my paycheck and I had three thousand dollars in it. When I reached the old lady on the phone, she said, "No problem," and before we blinked an eye, she brought it over. I saw her fly across the sky, do three backward somersaults over Zack's rooftop to land on my front porch—all four foot nine of her, and my wallet in hand. Then she said to me in that thick accent, "Be careful, Mr. Mayor, you lose your money, you lose your life."

THE BLOND SURFER DUDE

I've been working for the old lady since I was thirteen. I used to deliver for her on my bike. Then when my bike got stolen, I started delivering on my skateboard. Finally, she bought me a cool little Yamaha scooter for Christmas. My parents got divorced and my mother moved us up here from San Diego. She worked at the local drugstore and spent most of her time with bad boyfriends. So the old lady took me under her wing. She called me "number one," not because I'm her favorite, but because I've been at the restaurant the longest now and when I do kitchen work, I get the first shift. She can't pronounce my real name, which is Jeremy. So sometimes she calls me Jelly. After my grandmother died at the home, she said, "Call me Grandma Wong. I'm your grandma now."

Before I started to work for her, I heard all kinds of rumors, like she was chopping up people's dogs and eating them. That she was flying around and capturing bandits. That she knew black magic and caused a Diamond Reo to jackknife on Highway 5. The Fundamentalists here believe she's Satan. But she has always treated me like her own flesh. Let me tell you this. Once when I was doing kitchen duty with her in late afternoon, she and I were peeling shrimp together. Christ, we had a load of fresh Puget Sound shrimp, and we were peeling thousands of them. Only the two of us, because Nasty Marcus was allergic to shrimp blood. I said, "Asshole, shrimp don't have blood." But he said that he was allergic, that liar. He just wanted to sleep in that day. In any case, the old lady and I peeled away so that we could quick-freeze the shrimp before they spoiled. Then two enormous motherfuckers came through the kitchen door. One had a handgun with him. The other was so huge that he didn't need a gun—he had a bat. He came over and grabbed my hair and kneed me in the groin and then—*whack!* He hit my legs with the bat. The motherfucker broke my legs right then and there and I fell screaming. He stuffed a rag in my mouth and went into the banquet room to see if there were more people.

The other bastard put a gun to the old lady's head and said, "Where's the money, you old chink?" She said, "Not nice to break boy's leg," and before I saw it, she grabbed two sharp kitchen knives from the table and—*whish whish*—sliced off the gunman's hand. She was so fast he didn't see it coming. The gun flew off with the hand still holding it. He stood there staring at his stump gushing blood, screaming, "Fuck, fuck, you bitch." And the bastard who broke my leg came back and before he could think, she did a flying flail kick and popped him in the head. He fell backward over a pile of shrimp shells. She took his bat from him and whacked him again and again until he was out like a light. She stuffed his mouth with a bunch of shrimp because, she said, he used bad words. Then she called the police. Apparently, he almost died because he was allergic to shrimp. His whole face swelled up like a balloon. The other guy got his hand sewed back on by a famous hand surgeon like it was nothing.

Well, I took most of the credit for capturing the creeps. I guess they'd been on a spree, robbing small-town gas stations and truck stops and hurting people. I got a ten-thousand-dollar reward for being the hero. I put it in the bank for college. Grandma Wong won't take any of the credit. "The boy did it, the boy did it," she said. She put her finger to her lip to shush me. I think she didn't want people to know about her powers.

SCARS

Sometimes, after a long prosperous night, Grandma Wong would have a few drinks with her staff. Usually, the Chinese cooks would not join. They knew better than to show their vulnerable side to her. But, once in a while, she would sit and drink Vodka gimlets, straight up, without the twist (she wanted to save the extra rinds for her customers). This day she was celebrating her orange Manchurian carp's— Rice Cake's—fortieth birthday. She had smuggled him out of the labs in Guangdong when she was a biochemist for the People's Fish Ponds. She had experimented with genetic engineering to create the biggest food fish. Rice Cake was an ordinary orange carp, but he was also an important experiment. She and her team engineered him to be bigger and to live longer. He's a fifty-pound, forty-year-old carp. "He's my son I never had," she said, although everybody knew that she had a genetic human son who embezzled money from the accounts to pay for his gambling debts. "I think Buddha make joke: Men give you bad luck, so I give you two granddaughters and a fish."

That evening Surfer Dude proceeded to pour her a second gimlet and one for himself, and he didn't take the twist to show respect. He knew that the old lady was frugal about little things and he knew how to please her. Then Nasty Marcus, who would rather toke than drink, took a Bud. He knew not to take a Tsingtao because imports are more expensive. And Eric sipped an herbal green tea infusion that he and Grandma Wong had invented. (His father's an alcoholic, so Eric had sworn never to touch the stuff.) On special occasions, they would all sit around, relax and talk about various topics. The topic, then, was battle scars, to which the old lady had a lot to contribute. First of all, she was ancient. She had more years to accumulate wounds. Nobody actually knew how old she was. She would say, "Oh, I'm a hundred years old. I'm old enough to be your ancestor." Or "I'm ninety-five. Just one year older, my mother would have bound my feet." . . . "Oh, I hated those Manchus." . . . "Oh, I was the star of the Boxer Rebellion." Well, it would be impossible to date her. Her granddaughters decided that she was between 80 and 140.

After downing the second gimlet, she became very loud. She pulled up her trousers and showed off a large gouge on her inner left thigh covered by a patch of pink and purple shiny scar tissue. "One day, I came home from the fish pond. I was too tired to cook and I said to husband, 'Chairman Mao says that the sexes are equal, so you cook tonight.' My husband said, 'I no cook,' and he went to the kitchen and took out a cleaver and chased me around house. I throw salt in his eyes, kicked him in groin and he fell back, but I scrape leg against a broken hinge my husband not fix. I told him, 'You touch me again, I chop off head when you're asleep.' He was scared. He moved back to his mother. Then he brought me to trial for husband beating and I say no, I no beat him. He gambling roosters and got in fight. Then I showed the comrade officers my scar and they make him drop charges and let us divorce. Otherwise, they don't let divorce."

Marcus said, "Shit, it's a good thing that you knew how to defend yourself. He would have butchered you." Then Marcus pulled up his T-shirt. There was a small bullet scar down on his left hip. "I was delivering pizzas in Portland and a big long-haired greasy speed freak said, 'I ain't gonna pay you.' I said, 'Twenty-two fifty, asshole, or I'll call the cops.' He and his three chicks laughed at me and then he punched me in the face and took my money-belt with all the night's cash in it. I went back to the pizza truck and called the boss on the cell. The boss called the cops, and he told me to stay put until the cops come. When the cops came, the freak and his chicks had gone. Then the young rookie cop shot me. He thought that I was the bad guy cause I'm black."

The old lady inspected the scar and said, "You lucky, they could have shoot your kidney." Surfer Dude laughed, "Got you in the ass." The old lady laughed, "That's why you deliver Chinese food now and not pizza." There was a short silence after a few cackles, and then Eric stepped forward.

Eric pulled up his shirt. On his back, a huge rope of scars that turned into a giant oval shape covered his entire back. "Look closely," he said. "What's the matter, Marcus, did you flunk geography? It's the map of America." When the old lady got close and saw that the scar was actually a series of cigarette burns linked together in an attempt to make a map of the United States, she gasped and said, "Your father, no good, your father."

BIG BOY

You know we really thought that she was a vampire. Once, Surfer Dude took a picture of her, but her body didn't show up in the prints. Dude said, "I swear to God. I took a picture of her." Then we took a photo of the whole summer staff, and for some reason her face got cut out of the picture. All we got was her shoulder. So we decided that chink was really a vampire. I told my friends— Buz and Ralphie—about it and I decided that we should put a stake through her heart. You know, she sort of body-snatched the Dude, Eric and Marcus. They never come out anymore. They just hang around the restaurant. I worked the late shift and did mostly cleanup and vacuuming. She used to walk by and scowl at me. I said, "Do I stink or something?" But the old bitch never liked me. She told Marcus that she thinks I have an evil heart. She said that she saw disaster in my eyes. It really freaked me out when Marcus told me that. So I said to Buz, maybe she's a vampire, and she turned all those guys into baby vampires. I told some lies, that I saw her fly up to the giant tree and catch a squirrel in her teeth, suck its blood and throw its carcass in the garbage can. I found a roadkill and showed it to Ralphie for proof.

Then when Patsy and Ratsy's dog disappeared, I said that I saw the chink chop him up into moogoogaipan. When Eric's father disappeared, too, I said that I saw the old lady chop him up, put him in the meat-grinder and make dumplings out of him.

I said that every night she sucks blood from the necks of her granddaughters and that's why they don't age like white people do. They stay pretty. The mistake was wearing those stupid garlic bulbs. Buz, Ralphie and I went to the hardware store and got hammers and wooden stakes and strung garlic around our necks. She smelled us from miles away and ambushed us. She flung her broom around and broke my arm, donkey-kicked Ralphie unconscious, elbowed Buz in the ribs and knocked the wind out of him. She made those Bruce Lee yipping sounds, and—*bam, bam, bam*—we all went down. We were too ashamed to talk about this, to admit that a little old lady beat the shit out of us, so we told our parents that we got into a fight with some bad-ass Indian boys from Clackamas. She fired me the next day, and I ended up working at Safeway as a stock boy. Twenty years later and I'm still working there. That bitch put a hex on me. I'm stuck in Piss River, Oregon, forever.

ERIC THE RED

Mrs. Wong called me the red-haired demon because I had bright flaming Rastafarian kinky hair. It still sticks up like fire. Mrs. Wong made me wear a hairnet when I worked in the kitchen. I was studying a little Mandarin in college and some eastern religion and I took a semester off from Reed College because I was flunking all my classes and didn't know what I wanted to do. But Mrs. Wong was patient and taught me a few qigung exercises. I also liked rapping with her about plants and hydroponics. We were really good chums until I started falling in love with Mei Ling.

One day Mei Ling and I were messing around in the old

pigeon house on top of the restaurant roof. Mrs. Wong said she could smell my penis all the way from the beauty parlor, where she was having her weekly appointment. With curlers still in her hair, she flew out of the parlor and up to the roof, did a double backward somersault and threw a ninja star at me. I had my pants down around my ankles—still hot into it with Mei Ling. I wanted to pull up my pants as soon as I saw her airborne, but Mei Ling said, "Don't stop, fool, I haven't come yet. What are you, afraid of my little grandmother?"

The ninja star hit me, impaled my naked ass. The points were cured with some kind of sleeping herb that she grew in the garden. I immediately felt paralyzed and couldn't pull my pants up. My body was like rubber. I stayed there facedown on the roof for two hours. Mrs. Wong called my father at work and both my mother and father came to fetch me. They had to see me in this humiliating position, pants down, dick wilted, groggy and weak. My mother burst out in tears and called me a sinner and a degenerate. My father said, "Calm down, calm down, Mildred, let's not make a scene. The good Lord will take care of this." My mother stopped speaking to me, and my father kicked the shit out of me saying, "Praise God." I woke up the next day with three broken ribs and my eyes bruised and swollen shut.

I went back to the restaurant the next week and confessed to Mrs. Wong that I loved her granddaughter. I said, "I want to marry her and take her away from this terrible hellhole. We will run away to California and become rich and famous." She laughed so hard she popped a button from her blouse. Then she hardened her face and said, "You no love my granddaughter and my granddaughter no love you. You good boy, finish college, become somebody. Marry your own people and be happy." I said, "But I don't want to marry my own people, I don't like my own people." She pressed her little fist against my chest and said, "Go, marry your own people, don't come back."

THE RUMORS BUZZED

—I heard she cut off Eric's dick and cooked it in a curry stew and fed it to the Rosenblatts at table six.

—I heard she placed a restraining order against him for ten thousand years.

—I heard that when Surfer Dude smelled something terrible in the garbage can and saw Eric's dad's hand sticking out, it was bloody-purple, carved to the bone.

—I heard that it was Eric's father's eyeballs floating in Rusty Tallman's hot and sour soup.

—I heard that she put a hex on Eric's father and he turned into a zombie and drove his car to the edge of the St. John's Bridge in Portland and disappeared.

—They say she hated the fathers and forgave the sons, except for her own son, whom she could never forgive.

MING (THE SILENT COOK)

I came with one suitcase. My uncle and I tried to escape the Khmer Rouge, paying for passage aboard a pirate boat from Cambodia. I floated on this one suitcase and lived. So this is my lucky suitcase. The truth is this is not even my suitcase. It belonged to somebody named Ming, who drowned with my uncle and the others when the boat sprung open and sank. Ming had a green card, a clean suit and a letter from Grandma Wong to come to work as a cook in beautiful Rose River, Oregon. I got here and everybody calls it Piss River because the local paper mill has turned the place into a smelly, contaminated cesspool. The rain that falls all year round smells like piss.

When I got here, I was only thirteen. I couldn't speak Cantonese very well because I was raised in Cambodia. We spoke a different dialect. Grandma Wong was suspicious of me at first, but then she smiled and said, "Ming—Ming means bright. You will give us good luck and bring brightness into the restaurant." I was very happy to hear this because I didn't want her to call the INS and send me back. I would be killed with the rest of my family. They're killed because they're teachers. I come from a long line of teachers, and the Khmer Rouge hate teachers.

Apparently, Mrs. Wong's son embezzled over $100,000 from the restaurant payroll. He also took money from the mortgage but still couldn't pay for his gambling debt. So when he died suddenly, he left Grandma Wong with his debts and the Triads to contend with. These gangsters are from Macau, and they have Chinese Portuguese blood and they're really brutal. Grandma Wong knew that sooner or later, the gangsters would come to the restaurant to collect. Her guess was that they'd come to take all her money, then kill her and her granddaughters as a payback for her son's debts.

One day they wrote her and said they wanted $500,000. Otherwise, they would torch the restaurant and kill everybody in it. She set traps all over the house. Marcus and I made beds of nails for her, cured with a potion she made from deadly herbs. It took us all night to pound hundreds of nails into planks, with all the sharp points forming standing beds. Then Eric and I dug a huge "tiger pit" in the backyard and put five bags of lime in it. She sent her granddaughters to Salem to a friend's house. She gave all the rest of her workers a vacation, closed the restaurant, turned off all the lights at the circuit board and waited. I woke up in the middle of the night and I heard kicks and screams and gunshots. I tried to leave my room to help her, but she had locked me in. Two hours later, she knocked on my door. The bodies were too heavy for her, so I used a wheelbarrow and threw the bodies into the tiger pit.

Mrs. Wong and I both have secrets that bond us. Or perhaps we have enough evidence against each other so that if one breaks, the other would be destroyed. She would not ask about my real identity, and I will never again mention this incident. In gratitude, she built a little house in the back of the restaurant, with a bath and a kitchenette, for me to live in. She designed a nice skylight for the roof so that I could look up and see the heavens.

SINGING WAITRESS

(As Recorded by the Northwest Chinese American Oral History Project)

I was born on the road, burst into the world between Nanping and Fuzhou. My father was the manager of an acrobatic troupe. My mother was called the "pink contortionist." We went from town to town performing Peking opera skits for our supper. When I was small, I had a brilliant falsetto. My mother said, "You're my little sparrow. You will sing us out of poverty." But my father said, "You sound like a wounded deer. You'll bring predators to the table." My mother watched me all the time, fearful that my father would sell me or leave me in a faraway village. A girlchild was a burden on the road, just another mouth to feed.

The more we traveled, the more I sang. And with the coming of the Cultural Revolution, I became indispensable to the troupe because I sang our new nation's anthem, "The East Is Red, the Sun Is Rising." Madame Mao's people heard about my singing. So they cleaned me up, put rouge on my face, and I became the poster child of the Cultural Revolution. I recruited my gang of lost children and orphans, and we quickly rose to power. We put the grown-ups on trial. I loved putting a dunce cap on my father's head and shouting, "Traitor Hound, Decadent Rightist!" I made my father get on his bare knees and confess his guilt. I would make him pay for hating me all those years. We sent him to hard labor camp and never heard from him again. After the sentencing, they placed all the prisoners on an oxcart. When my mother ran after the cart to see him off, her shirt got caught in the spokes and she was dragged for half a mile before she was finally killed.

I didn't shed a tear for my mother or my father. I was bold and ignorant then. I led my band of orphans all over the small towns of China, waving red books and slashing the faces of Buddhas. Then the tides changed again. Our protectorate, Madame Mao, was arrested with the Gang of Four—and the Cultural Revolution was over. My small band of hoodlums had to beg from town to town for food. Somehow, we ended up in Guangdong and a group of elderly peasants started beating us with brooms and hoes. My friends scattered to the four winds, but I was too sick and hungry to leave and I sat in a ditch for three days, waiting to die. A man's giant shadow hovered over me and said, "Dog Puke, Pig Rot! Where is your Madame Mao now?" He picked me up from the ditch and smuggled me to Hong Kong to be a sex slave.

He passed me on from cathouse to cathouse and I was forced to have sex with at least twenty men a night.

I met Auntie Wu at a cathouse on Christopher Street called The Cage. She lived in the flat straight across from the waiting room. One day she heard me singing on the balcony an ancient folksong that my Hakka grandmother taught me. "We are both from the same tribe," she said, then climbed out of her window and onto my balcony and sang with me. That afternoon, I told her the story about my sad life and she held my hand and said, "Don't blame yourself, girlchild. History is filled with ruts and fissures. It's time to make a new Long March!"

The next week, Auntie Wu brought me a large envelope. It was a perfect escape kit with detailed instructions, a fake passport, a tourist visa, a ticket to Portland, Oregon, and a Greyhound bus ticket to Rose River. She also included a bamboo straw, ten blow-darts cured with sleeping potion and a manual called "The Secrets of the Snake Escape." I studied the secret manual closely and did snake exercises every day to condition my body.

On the night of September 19, on the tail of the Moon festival, I made my escape. Exactly at midnight, I took my bamboo straw and blew a dart into the night watchman's thigh. He quickly fell into a deep sleep. Then I made myself into a snake and crawled out between the bars of the window. With one change of clothing, my fake passport and my airline ticket stuffed in my large tote bag, I took a cab to the airport and began my new life.

At the Rose River terminal, a short Chinese girl with a shaved head came up to me and said in bad Mandarin, "Welcome, I am Little Sister Moon." She was holding a large white sign with bright gold Chinese characters on it that said "Double Happiness Restaurant." This made me smile with all my heart. I sighed, "Finally, I've reached paradise." But how curious Americans are. When I asked her, "The slogan on the back of your T-shirt, what does it say?" She laughed and said, "Eat Shit and Die."

MING AND MEI LING

I must tell you about me and Mei Ling. For some reason, that little girl took a liking to me. We were friends from the start. I was eighteen, getting trained as a cook. She was thirteen, cute and quick and fresh as a flower in her little red hapi coat. When she was not at the cash register guiding customers in, she was at a side table folding napkins or making wontons. She had beautiful little hands and when she was not folding, she read and did her homework. Sometimes, she would sit with me and help me with my English lessons.

But something happened when she turned sixteen. They say a ripening peach cannot know its own dangerous sweetness. She started wearing skimpy dresses and paraded around the boys. All of us in the kitchen were afraid. If anything went wrong, the old lady would deport us or flay us alive.

Mei Ling loved to tease me. She'd walk into my little room in the back of the restaurant to ask for a pencil. I knew very well that she had her own pencils, and she would rub past me. Her perky little breasts and her sweet smell would make me dizzy. I would turn my head and not say anything. One day, she said, "Look, my sweet cousin, look and look hard," and suddenly she was naked before me. She put her little perfect fingers on her little mound and started stroking herself. I quickly turned away. From then on, I locked the door to my room and didn't open when she called.

Then she slipped notes under the door. They were little sexy love poems: "Roses are red, violets are blue, your cock is pretty and I love you." The poems were both childish and pornographic. I knew that I shouldn't keep them. If the old lady found out, she would kill me. But I couldn't throw them away. I kept every one of them. I wanted to possess them as I wanted to possess Mei Ling.

I put all her little poems into my lucky suitcase. Sometimes, when I was sad, I would pull the suitcase out from under the bed to reread the poems and go through the few things that belonged to the real Ming. I have taken the identity of this poor boy who was much prettier than I and much smarter. In the suitcase was a class photo taken in Phenom Phen. He was the healthy, happy one in the middle. There was a blue ribbon he won for an essay contest. The beautiful suit that I kept perfectly folded and starched is now a little moldy. I still hug it and cry quietly into it.

I can't imagine where the real Ming is, under the ocean perhaps, fishes living in his cavities. Or he's in heaven with my parents playing mahjong. I feel sad for him and for myself. I wonder how fate has brought us into these worlds. How is it that he has drowned and I have survived? Am I really alive? I feel dead, smothered in this little dying town. Day in and day out, I wake carving flesh and reeking of stale soy sauce. I greet the same stars when I open my door to the kitchen in the morning, and I say goodnight to the same stars when I go to sleep. They don't seem to want to change their pattern. The long days in between are blurs. My body aches from swinging the knife, and my ears burn with the shrieks of sizzling woks.

The white kids that work in the kitchen come and go in the summer. The kitchen was like a train stop. They would leave eventually for a better destination. Some of them would send postcards from their universities or exotic places. The undocumented, the unidentified, the brown boys paid under the table—we all call little brother, cousin. They, too, keep moving, changing. They move from sweatshop to sweatshop, from kitchen to groves. One ended up in the Piss River and Mrs. Wong had to go to the morgue and identify the body. "He was a good boy," she said.

. . .

Mei Ling, when I reread the little poems, I remember how I loved you. You were a complete mystery. Your grandmother told me to stay away from you, that you were a fox girl and that you had inherited the fleshly desires from your vixen mother. That you would doom any man that touches you. But in those early years of the restaurant, you were the glimmer of hope in my life. When I heard you giggle or saw you doing your homework, reading great Western literature, or merely sitting in the corner with your sister and your friends, how your intense focus could flitter into sparrows. How American life could seem so comfortable.

Tomorrow, I will not be alive. I will put on Ming's moldy suit—and walk into the river with stones sewn into my pockets.

MING, REDUX

One day, I thought about killing myself, but at the last minute I changed my mind. When I walked into the river with stones in my pockets, I heard frogs croaking on the fragrant banks. I remembered my childhood near the Mekong River and how I enjoyed hearing the frogs at night. They cry "love, love." I turned around and walked home in a brief calm between rains under a full moon. The highway was black and empty except for a bright white line that disappeared in the horizon. I was happy to see the restaurant's neon flickering in the distance. I changed my wet clothes and went to the kitchen to prep for a twenty-course dragon and phoenix banquet. One hundred ducks were waiting to be dressed. Ten thousand shrimps sang to be eaten. I found peace in dicing carrots, calm in slicing onions, dignity in carving rosettes out of common radishes.

The next year, Grandma Wong legally adopted me and sent me to Oregon State at Corvallis, where I got a degree in agricultural science. I took over her little hybrid experiments, and we started a huge organic agribusiness together. We have a seaweed farm down near Coosbay and an experimental salmon run in Tillamook.

Once in a while I see Mei Ling, and we laugh about the silly pornographic poems that she used to send me. She's now a poet/professor in southern California who is well-known for her research on immigrant erotica. I said to her, "Well, you had a good start." Remembering how flirty she was, she blushed. Every year for spring break, she would fly up to Corvallis for a visit. We would have tea together and laugh a bit, and I would give her a check from the business because in Grandma Wong's will, she named all of us, Marcus, Surfer Dude, the singing waitress, Mei Ling, Moonie, and I, equal partners. Mei Ling is as mysterious and untouchable now as she was at thirteen. I know that I can never know her again. The country is vast and each of us, frogs in our own ponds. And poor Rice Cake. He fell ill shortly after Grandma Wong's death, died of a broken heart. We buried him at a bend of the river.

RICE CAKE CARP SONG

I am a fish, a big fat fish, I have no father or mother
I am a fish, a big fat fish, I am spawn from an ancient river
I am a fish, a big fat fish, I grow fatter and fatter
Each day I munch on tasty scraps, handfed by my sisters
Each night I sleep in my sooty bed unafraid of anglers
Flay me, eat me, I am eternal flesh
I'll reborn myself over and over
I'll return to earth as a big fat fish
To feed the Great Hunger

PATSY AND RATSY
(Patricia and Rebecca, twins)

We hate Mei Ling and Moonie. We had to grow up in their shadows. They were always straight A students. We were B– students. Our mother always said, "Why can't you be smart like Mei Ling and Moonie?"

One day our dog, Maggie, disappeared and we told the police that their grandmother chopped him up and ate him. And Ralphie witnessed it. This made them start an investigation and the animal rights crazies found out and picketed their restaurant. They had to close it for a month. Then one day somebody in Spokane found Maggie and took down the number from her collar and called us. Apparently, she took a ride on a northeast-bound freight train and ended up four hundred miles away in Spokane. How weird is that? We were suspended from school for spreading malicious rumors.

When old Granny Wong died, our father and his corporation tried to buy the property. They wanted to tear the restaurant down and build a shopping mall. Mei Ling and Moonie refused to deal with us and ended up selling it very cheap to a Vietnamese family. My father said, "How do you like that, gooks will only do business with gooks."

MARCUS MARCUS

One day, Grandma Wong caught a cold and died. They said they looked at her birth certificate and she was actually 124 years old. Although she was a lifelong Buddhist, we had a quiet Christian ceremony for her because we couldn't find a Buddhist priest in the yellow pages. The dude and I took time from college to be there. Eric was there quietly weeping behind a tree because there is still a restraining order against him to stay a thousand feet away from Mei Ling. When Mei Ling and Moonie walked up to the gravesite, Moonie was so absorbed in trying to capture the funeral with her hand-cam that she tripped over a headstone and fell into a nearby ditch. Grandma Wong's ghost sprang out of her coffin, pulled Moonie from the ditch and said, "You must rise up, girl-child, you must change the world!" She then flew into the trees. And there she is. A silhouette between moon and branches, she sings to us every night—a Chinese song that is soft and soothing. You can hear her precisely at midnight when she would normally be turning off the neon signs of the restaurant. She must have put a spell on all of us. Because the song she sings is a fuckin' sad song. Although we don't understand a word of it, it makes us all cry when we hear it.

RESTAURANT SESTINA

They have all gone away. The restaurant is shut and still. There's noth-
ing left to say. The abacus is idle. Silent is the till. They have all gone
away. Mei Ling is here for just a day. Moonie pays the rest of the bills.
Nothing more to say. The Old Lady planned it just this way. The symbol
of toil and love, they shall sell, sell. They have all gone away. They've
sold it to Mrs. Pham, the restaurant on the hill. There's nothing left to
say. Only the crying cockroaches will stay. The restaurant is shut and
still. We have all gone away. Nothing left to say.

. . .

Sign off: Marcus Marcus, poet/anarchist, celestial skateboarder,
fool.

COCKROACH LATE-SONG

A brown girl is as juicy as a white girl, although an old lady is less so,
she's the first to let go. Ho, Ho, Ho! Bits of meat on the carpet, pretty
little morsels, sweet and sour to my nose. Ho, Ho, Ho! A brown girl's as
juicy as a white girl, although an old lady's less so: be patient, be patient,
I can smell her cooking through the mouse hole. She's wokking up some
old rice with egg and scallion, she'll drop a few crumbs behind the stove.
Na na na, we're fast we're bold, we'll escape her broom and foot-soles.
Ho, Ho, Ho! Our kind is hard, our kind is patient, hold the door, hold
the door.

Our cousins are coming. Here come the uncles. We have our green cards,
our underground passes, our fake photos. Ho, Ho, Ho! Our ancestors are

older than your ancestors! One dead cockroach is a tragedy, ten million is a statistic! Ho, Ho, Ho!

Our kind will be patient, patient. We'll crawl in and out of her ears, in and out of her nostrils, in and out of her eyeholes. Ho, Ho, Ho! First, we'll take over the restaurant, then take over the world. Ho, Ho, Ho! We are courageous, we're bold, we're not afraid of your foot-soles!

MEI LING LAST SONG

How is it that some of us go away and some of us stay? Some sink into the ocean and some ride a dead man's suitcase to safety. Some of us are beautiful Chinese girls who don't age, or dishwashers who die with hands soft as a baby's.

Perhaps the only bright light in a dying western town may be the neon of a Chinese restaurant. Perhaps that same bright light may be a take out joint in Bethlehem.

Some of us are born with wings and some of us crawl on our bellies. Some of us could spin shit into gold. Some of us pan and pan and come up empty.

Some of us are Chinese from China. Some of us from Africa, from Vietnam and Cambodia, from Timbuktu, from Andalusia—the whole world is our diaspora.

Some of us arrive in the promised land. Some of us land in Piss River, Oregon. Glittering sand, putrid rain, it's all the same to us.

Some of us love too much and some of us don't love much at all. Some of us, like Mei Ling, love the wrong people, over and over. Some of us, like Moonie, wary Moonie, prefer to keep the score. And who is to say who loves whom more?

Some of us work our knuckles black. Some of us sleep facing the stars.

Some of us are prized fish. Some of us are common swine raised for slaughter.

Some of us are like Mei Ling, or we are more like her than we would like to admit—although we have plenty, we cry more, more, more. . . .

Happiness: A Manifesto

I'm not sure I'm adult yet.

—*Johnny Depp*

When you realize how perfect everything is, you will tilt your head back and laugh at the sky.

—*Buddha*

A Zygote's Confession

When I was just a singular zygote, floating in my mother's amniotic fluid, happy in my self-assured way, I had no idea that on the second day in the world I would divide into two separate embryos and have to share the placenta with my silly sister, Mei Ling. Back then, Mother was working two jobs, day time as a clerk at a motel, night time at the failing family restaurant.

One day, she was tired and bitchy after the ultrasound. She said, "Oh Buddha, let me die. I don't want twins! Kill one of them!" She had to be hospitalized twice after bleeding episodes, and my father, red-faced and greasy from a twelve-hour shift from the restaurant, said, "It's all your fault. You've been eating too much duck." She replied, "Idiot, when do I have time to chew on duck?!" Then, story has it, she threw a butcher knife at him and it missed his head and stuck itself—*boing*—dead-centering a tintype of one of our beloved ancestors. This would mean bad luck for eternity.

I heard them argue every night, the precocious blob that I was, and arrogant too. I was but a thought the size of a thumbnail, though possessing an ego of megalomaniac proportions. "I'll try to help you, Mommy," I yelled and declared that I would kill

Mei Ling. I squeezed my umbilicus with all my might and tried to suck the very blood out of her. The doctor called it "twin to twin transfusion syndrome" or TTTS. He brought in specialists and medical students to examine my condition. I did not have bad intentions. I merely was honoring my poor, tired mother's wishes. It's beside the point that I wanted the womb all to myself. I was already exhibiting humanness with self-serving tendencies.

And Mei Ling just floated in the placenta, eyes closed. She said nothing. Of course not, we're supposed to be unconscious blobs, floating safely in the primeval universe of the womb. We're supposed to be helpless in the midst of reincarnation, delighting in the transitory state between "being and not being," the process of "becoming." We're supposed to be protected and yet to be exposed to the world of rampant greed and tribal violence, still unaware of the child molester who lives upstairs and the suicide bomber waiting around the corner.

After a third bleeding episode, my mother was in so much pain she screamed, "I hate America. I want to go home to Hong Kong! I want to go back to my mother." My father yelled, "Go ahead, we'll abort the two-headed demon, pickle it in a jar and show it at the circus and make a million dollars so that we won't have to work like dogs anymore! You can go back to Hong Kong, crawl back into your mother's womb and be reborn again as a cockroach!"

They fought throughout the entire pregnancy. How can two exhausted immigrants muster up so much hatred toward one another?! Perhaps, even negative passion is better than no passion at all. Their lack of emotional control disgusted me. They're supposed to be disciplined: stoic Chinese people that never crack a smile or a grimace. The enemy shouldn't be able to tell if you're in ecstasy or in pain.

My grandmother intervened and said, "Shhh, don't you know that twin girls mean twin happiness? They will give us good luck. You'll see. The restaurant will turn around and be successful." She would rub my mother's belly and say, "Don't fight any more. The unborn will hear you from the womb. The ancestors will hear you from the grave."

After my grandmother's consoling and cutting-edge medical attention from the specialists, my homicidal urges abated, and I decided to stop bleeding my twin. In short, once again, I manifested my God complex and let Mei Ling live, which gave my mother a reprieve from terrible pains until our caesarian birth day. The Doc cut my mother open and yanked me out feet first, and I bawled and bawled—*wa wa wa*. Then Mei Ling came out smiling like the village idiot, or perhaps she was just high on the epidural. "Hmmm," the Doc said, "an optimist and a pessimist. A yin and a yang."

"Thanks for showing your Oriental knowledge, asshole," I shouted and peed on him. A stream of gingery broth oozed down his scrubs.

. . .

My parents stopped arguing, but what ensued after the rage was deadly silence. My mother spent most of her spare moments of our childhood facing the wall, sobbing. She had postpartum depression big-time. She refused to feed us or caress us. When she was not sobbing, she was sleeping. Our best memory of her was a sighing lump under the blanket. Meanwhile, my father continued to work like a dog and at night, after all his chores, started gambling on horses, dogs, cocks, bullfrogs, dice, cards for that Chinaman's chance for happiness. He died of a massive heart attack facedown in a tub of fermenting tofu, leaving my grandmother a mountain of gambling debts. My mother was inconsolable after that and flew back to Hong Kong, never to return.

. . .

There is no empirical evidence that our parents' sacrifice was worth it. Thirty years later, Mei Ling and I lived on opposite coasts. She was in Boston, studying for her second PhD, this time in literature. I was working in a prestigious biotech lab in California. We talked over webcam every night at precisely eleven eastern time. Her face would float up on my screen, chattering about everything and nothing: a Jimmy Choo shoe sale at Saks, a couple of racist colleagues whom she wants to castrate. She wants to dress up as a ninja and gut her ex-husband. She wants to dress *me* up as a ninja and gut her ex-boyfriend. Her new barista boytoy's got a great bod but writes bad poems. Kid No. 1's teeming brain, Kid No. 2 has new sublingual braces . . . Iraq, Iran. The burqa and the yashmak—are they one and the same? Is a toga a Roman version of a sarong? What killed third-wave feminism and whence ended compassionate socialism? And how are we culpable?

I listened to her babbling every night, thinking I should have let her die in the womb. My world would be much quieter now. All I want anymore is quiet. After midnight, I like to put on my earphones and look into my microscope: There is peace in flesh-eating bacteria, calm in deadly and benign spirochetes. The beings swim around in adagio, multiply gracefully to Chopin. They don't talk back. They're amoral creatures. No ill intentions belie their actions. No judgment intercedes, whether they cure or kill.

Most nights, there is perfect control from the Moon's eye view. Though, once in a while, at the hour of the rat, I have certain nostalgic pangs. Tonight, I retrieve from the deep freeze an old slide of Mei Ling's first yeast infection, labeled "Summer of 1999, Millennium, Killer Itch." I magnify it to the max and sadly contemplate the design.

How splendid, how ridiculous, that despite everything, I am inextricably bound to and am deeply in love with this silly human being.

Singing Worm

After twenty years of postponing her love life and toiling as a professor of immunology at Caltech, Moonie finally has a breakthrough. She has been studying the humoral and cellular system of an earthworm named Carlos for fifteen years. Carlos is not just any worm. Carlos's immune system is so strong that Moonie can bombard it with legions of aggressive invader organisms, and Carlos fends them off. But what's truly remarkable about this worm is that while gobbling up intruders like a worthy ninja, it screeches out the first famous bars of Beethoven's Fifth Symphony. This discovery was both too sublime and too ridiculous to countenance at first though Carlos's performances are uniformly sustained and ever nonpareil. Nevertheless, Moonie has not had the guts to disclose this virtuosity to her colleagues, not even to her assistants, lest they think she is a lunatic. So until she can wrap up her empirical conclusions, she has confined the worm to her personal lab in the basement of her house.

· · ·

After finishing up another exhausting semester battling with her colleagues about the recent cuts in the budget, Moonie flies to

Beijing to be a part of an immunity panel at the World Health Organization conference. There, she comes upon a striking six-foot-tall biochemist—a half-Chinese, half-Mongolian beauty named Maggie May Wu, who teaches at Beijing University. (Yes, her mother was once one of Chou En-lai's drivers and got wind of that lugubrious song by Rod Stewart over Radio Free Europe airwaves during an ad hoc trip to Xinjiang Province. Thus was bestowed Maggie May's unfortunate name.) She stands there, arms crossed, in her perfect Kabuki bob haircut: tawny, skinny, legs up to her neck. "Dr. American Moonie Genius Shortstuff," she says, "let's go to my apartment and have wild sex!" Therefore, after Moonie's talk, they skip a couple of panels on sub-Saharan diseases, make exquisite passionate romping in Maggie's twentieth-story apartment and afterward, gobble down two bowls of steamy veggie dumplings at the corner noodle shop.

The second day of their love affair, Maggie drives Moonie around in her antique pink Vespa, showing her all the must-see tourist spots in Beijing. At the Forbidden Palace, she says, "You have nothing majestic enough to rival this in your feudal American past." At the Great Wall, she scoffs, "If Bush had gonads, he would erect something of this scale to keep out the Mexican barbarians." At the National Stadium, she declares, "We're going to destroy you American blowhards and squish you like gnats at the Olympics!" By late afternoon, Moonie is sick of Maggie's competitive jousting. She feels like yelling *redguardsredguardsredguards* or *gangoffourgangoffourgangoffour* to remind Maggie May of China's recent historical failings. However, for the sake of international peace, she keeps her mouth shut, and besides she wants more sex before she leaves this wretched, polluted city.

At a quieter moment, over a glass of soothing bubble tea, Moonie divulges to Maggie the pending blockbuster, her singing worm Carlos, thinking that Maggie would be impressed. Maggie, however, yawns and says, "Dr. American Moonie Genius Short-stuff, I'm sorry to say that your experiment is a pittance. You must come to my lab at Beijing University, and I shall show you truly *sublime* creatures."

So they Vespa to a brand new lab that put all of Caltech to shame. The size of a football stadium, the lab shows the prowess of the new medical research wing. Gleaming white walls, stainless-steel counters, brand new equipment, Maggie May's lab makes Moonie's look like a medieval dungeon.

Maggie escorts Moonie to a vast smelly room filled with noisy animals in cages. There she points out her "sublime creatures": a two-headed goose that honks Frost's "Mending Wall" in stereo; a cloned goat that *baas* the best hits of the Confucian Odes; a Hummer-size immortal butterfly who mocks Zhuangzi; a 302-year-old tortoise who belts out the aria "Pace, pace mio Dio" from *La Forza del Destino* in full-throated soprano. Finally, Maggie introduces a lizard-looking animicula from the Amazon, yet to be classified, which might possess the enzymes that inhibit the neural transmitters of pain. Maggie pouts and pets its head with a mocking tone of sadness. "This is my favorite creature, No. C2AH2354905. Someday, it will cure the world from suffering." But the poor bard has a compulsive disorder. No. C2AH2354905 just sits in the corner babbling nonstop Wordsworth from its slimy purple orifice.

After ten minutes or so of listening to the creature, Moonie grows impatient and finally breaks her silence. "*Oh lord, Jesus-MaryHolyBuddhaKrishna,*" Moonie shouts, "the stupid reptile has no artistic discernment. It can't stop itself from reciting *all* of Wordsworth! How can it save the world if it can't mitigate its own suffering?!"

Moonie refuses her last Vespa ride and takes a gypsy cab back to the hotel. Maggie tries to call Moonie's room several times for a last good-bye conversation, but Moonie mutes the ringer and does not pick up. She feels relieved to get away from the braggadocio giantess and has no intentions of speaking to her again.

Moonie sleeps through most of her long flight home. When she arrives at her doorstep, trellises of California jasmine greet her with their knock-out sweet scent. A battalion of hummingbirds flit about competing for the best nectar. Verbena and hibiscus flash vibrant yellow and crimson. Her entire yard is brilliantly alive. Once in the house, she takes a refreshing shower, pours a cup of white tea and slips into her comfy Hello Kitty pj's. She skims through her telephone messages, most of which are from Mei Ling and various associates from the lab, and to her surprise, two amorous hot and sexy breaths from Maggie and then a joke whose punch line got lost in the translation. (*This is President George . . . Oh my, they are all named George, aren't they? There are two in the Bush and one crossing the Delaware, ha ha ha!*) Moonie calls back and leaves *Meow Meow Mao Mao Mao Mao* on Maggie's machine. She has to succumb to the idea that this might turn out to be an interesting long-distance relationship.

Moonie erases the messages to begin a fresh memory, shrugs on her favorite psychedelic tie-dyed lab coat and walks down to her basement lab. And there to greet her is her paramour Carlos, who has sprouted four new heads during her absence. They crane their tiny pink necks upward and belt out several verses of "Ode to Joy." Unfortunately, after a fine streak of spontaneous "hallelujahs," they lose their perfect a cappella harmony and devolve into some ghastly fingernails-on-the-chalkboard yawping toward God.

The Ghost of Pig-Gas Illusions

For Moonie's thirtieth birthday, Mei Ling gave her a new pair of very expensive progressive Dolce&Gabbana glasses. They have shiny black frames with little rhinestones on the outer rims. Too girly-girl diva for Moonie's edgy style, but she decided not to exchange them following Mei Ling's fashion advice to dress up the drab lab coat world. Though as soon as Moonie put them on, the ghost of her grandmother appeared wearing a soy sauce–stained wife-beater T-shirt, flannel Mickey Mouse pj bottoms and waving her favorite forge-iron cleaver. She shouted, "I'm going to flay you, you pig-rot, dog-puke, ungrateful poop-maggot, reactionary, rightist, money-monger!"

"Hang that cleaver back on the wall, Grandmother. You can't flay me," Moonie shouted back. "You're dead, and I'm alive and shining."

After this exchange, the apparition vanished. Then Moonie decided that the turmoil must be in the new glasses. Her sister's a mean little fox with many tricks up her sleeve. So Moonie took off her glasses and put in her contacts and drove to work. She'd deal with her trickster sister later. At the lab, she went to her office to answer her messages, then conducted a two-hour meeting in the conference room.

And again her grandmother appeared, waving her giant cleaver and hanging on a raft of florescent lights left-handed like an agile chimpanzee. "You need a good flaying, you bamboo-shoot half wit! You think you're powerful! You think that these white people actually are giving you power, ha ha ha!"

Moonie looked around the lab to make sure that nobody else saw this apparition. This would be very embarrassing. Your ghost grandmother, waving a giant cleaver at you, shouting in archaic Chinese, wearing a wife-beater T-shirt and Mickey Mouse flannels, while you are supposed to be director of a bio lab at a distinguished university. But nobody seemed to notice. They are all self-absorbed monomaniacs in the first place, focused obsessively on their own agendas. They don't give a damn about much else.

After the meeting adjourned, the grandmother ghost followed Moonie from the lab to the parking lot, slumped in the back seat of Moonie's car and continued her name-calling, "Empty gourd, horse fertilizer!" Moonie turned on the radio full-blast to a hard-rock station. The bass rattled her teeth, but her grandmother ghost continued her vitriolic assault. "Idiot Princess, wretched eunuch, scion of pig-gas illusions! One flick of an eyelash and you've destroyed the kingdom!"

Why was her grandmother ghost so angry? Why had she returned to harass her? She'd been dead for several years now. Moonie and Mei Ling had taken care of all the family business. They exacted all her wishes—sold and divided, liquidated and banked appropriately and expeditiously. Of course, Moonie did not expect to resolve her dilemma soon. An old Chinese woman's anger is a god-given right. You cannot extinguish it even in the grave. Consider yourself lucky if a cleaver-wielding grandmother ghost doesn't break the beams of your roof, or set your house afire, or curse you with a crippling and disfiguring disease.

When Moonie got to her house, she slammed the door in the ghost's face. For a little while, the ghost went away. Moonie took a long shower to contemplate her options should the grandmother ghost come back.

Moonie thought: I cannot gouge out my eyes. I cannot sit in the dark of this room hoping that her apparition won't appear. I can't go on letting her dominate my life from the grave. And that archaic Taishan dialect is hard on the ears: cacophonic, accusatory and downright malicious and abusive. Indeed, Granny was a dominant bitch when she was alive. She was a thousand times mightier in death.

After warming up day-old Chinese food from the local Panda fast-food joint and pouring herself a cup of oolong tea, Moonie booted up her laptop. Her grandmother's wide-angle face appeared on the webcam. "I know you're trying to get rid of me forever," said the ghost. "You're an ungrateful child. Dead bag of girl bones, four-legged, sperm-killing animicula! I refuse to leave. And all your CIA war machines and FBI agents can't oust me!"

As in the past, the only way to escape the situation was to sit in the dark with the lights out and put on her earphones. Moonie and Mei Ling were masters at blocking their grandmother out. As a result, they both have an enormous CD collection and are developing early deafness. Moonie put on the latest compilation of old school soul—*ooo baby baby*—to be followed by hours of Tibetan throat singing and Gregorian chants.

She could still hear the grandmother apparition in muffled tones. But not seeing her in that ghastly T-shirt and flannel bottoms was a relief. The accusatory words still flickered in and out of her earphones in bad translation: "Butterfly crap! What are you flitting around for? Beetle dung on the bottom of my slippers, when will you rise up and help your people? You think I don't know your intentions! One dead brown girl is a tragedy, ten thousand is a statistic! You learned nothing from feudalism. You call that poetry? Why don't you memorize the three hundred poems of the Tang? You call that Chinese cooking? Sweet and sour gonads? The sauce is redder than pig's blood? The rape of Nanking was your fault! The Boxer Rebellion was not quite a rebellion, was it? Ssu-ma Ch'ien sacrificed his pee-pee for the likes of you! A thousand years of bound feet and still, you don't know the escape route!"

The ghost continued to rant, climbed out of the laptop and splayed herself out on the loveseat.

"Have you ever been stoned to death for a crime you did not commit? Have you ever been torched in flames because your husband desires a better dowry?

"Do you call that love? What do you know about unconditional love? Have you carried your dead mother on your back for ten miles to find the perfect burial ground? Have you opened your daughter's ribs to carve out her infected appendix with a rusty blade? Have you placed your body over your baby, so that the bullets would hit you first? Have you ever carried your sick child on your back and begged from village to village for medicine? (Meanwhile, the vultures are flapping overhead and the jackals are biting your heels.) Have you ever been sold by your own heroin-addicted father to the sex trade? Tell me, American brat, what do you know about sacrifice?"

The drone had colluded with the throat singing and made Moonie doze off. She woke up to find the ghost snoring on her side, cheek to her cleaver.

. . .

Perhaps Moonie will succumb to the possibility that she will never be rid of this ghost, that she has to sit in the dark with her glasses off and blast her mind out with loud music to assuage this unbearable pain. She has to come around to the idea, too, that she is tied to her personal limitations. But Mei Ling would be quick to point out that apathy is a choice, not a limitation. And with perfect 20/20, Mei Ling, at the ripe age of forty, dances in clubs with boy-toys every Saturday night. She tells Moonie to "Chill out, sister, you're an American. Don't you know that an unexamined life is worth living and worth living well?"

Perhaps, as time goes on and when Moonie finally confesses to the grandmother ghost about her unbearable loneliness, the apparition will fade away as memory fades. The wife-beater T-shirt, in its abstracted form, won't look so tawdry. The Mickey Mouse pj's too won't seem so mocking and embarrassing. All might fade into the white cloud-vault of history. All the aphorisms, parallel phrases, vivid name-calling and historical rage would blend into the tunes of her massive and eclectic playlist.

By and by, perhaps, her grandmother's mighty cleaver will be re-imagined and re-smithyed into wind chimes, and the sharpness of her grandmother's unsparing tongue will soften into distant poetry.

Parable of the Guitar

O nce upon a time there were two young lovers. He was a skillful guitarist, she was a skillful listener. He, an aspiring musician, practiced day and night. She didn't mind sitting across from him, cross-legged for hours. So in love was she that it didn't matter that he was in the midst of creating an original composition, or just practicing chords or deep into his own thoughts. She was utterly happy to abandon herself to him and subjugate herself to be his perfect listener.

The guitarist said, "Listen, Mei Ling, a trickling spring . . ." He would move the plectrum across the strings lightly, and Mei Ling would reply, "Yes, I can hear it, yes, trickling, trickling every drop of quiet water. The beautiful stream soothes me." "This one is called 'Pearls on a Jade Plate,'" he continued. "Yes, I can imagine, pearls rolling gentling on blue celadon. I can see the décor of the Forbidden Palace, and a fresh, pink-cheeked concubine walking toward us gingerly, on lotus feet," she said, mocking him gently.

"This one is called 'Panning for Gold,'" he said. To this she replied, "Yes, I can see my ancestors swishing, swishing the nuggets in their pans. They are squatting at the riverbank, scorching under the blaring sun, their long queues sticking to their sweaty backs."

He said, "Listen, from the west, thunderclap and lightning." His fingers sliding up and down the shiny muscular neck of the guitar, his plectrum fast and furious. "Yes, I can hear it," she said, muffling her ears. "I am frightened. It makes me want to crawl into bed and hide under the covers."

He continued, "Can you hear the railroad, the train coming from the distance?" She said, "Yes, yes, I can see and hear it, the approaching train. It comes all the way from Plymouth Rock to settle in the wild west. I can see my ancestors toiling, laying the tracks. They're shouldering pickaxes, giant mallets and shovels."

"This one is called, 'The Five Horses of the Apocalypse.'"

"Yes, yes, but only five? Shouldn't there be ten? I suppose a half-baked apocalypse is better than none."

They would go on this way for hours. He would strum for her; she would respond with playful, cheeky remarks. It was a healthy bantering between two young lovers. He was proud of his political awareness and his new male, feminized sensitivity. She was deeply in love with his hard body and his youthful intensity. She believed in his talent and had faith in their future together. She would postpone her own aspirations to write the great American novel. (In fact, she stopped short on page 124, the immigrant chapter, right when the protagonist was about to pour tea.) Instead, Mei Ling went back to school to get her second PhD and ended up teaching at the local college; meanwhile, she also joined a cadre of lawyers who represented migrant workers at the Calexico border. She didn't mind working hard; she was intent on supporting her man through both his PhD dissertation and his dreams of becoming a consummate guitar master.

. . .

Their love affair went on for years in front of the hearth. Sometimes she would oil the guitar for him or buy him extra strings. And on his fortieth birthday, she bought him a fancy rhinestone-studded case from a celebrity auction. Supposedly, it was once owned by Elvis Costello. It cost her $5,000, but she felt that it was worth every cent. From then on, he and the rhinestone-studded case would be inseparable. He would carry it everywhere he went. It was the emblem of his art and a precious gift from the woman who cherished him.

· · ·

"Does this sound like Hendrix at Monterey Park?" he pondered aloud. She answered, "Yes, yes, I can see you there, on stage, setting the guitar on fire. You, in an Afro, purple velvet bandana. The crowd is wild, half naked, writhing, stoned out of their minds. Oh burning, burning genitals! Oh burning Hendrix genitals!" Her mockery embarrassed him. Sometimes, he didn't know whether she was merely being silly or was being aggressively ironic.

"And this, does this sound just like Clapton's 'Layla' in his Derek and the Dominos years?" he inquired. "Yes, it was a song inspired by his passion for George Harrison's wife, wasn't it?" Though Mei Ling was more a Hendrix fan and found "Layla" a little redundant, she enjoyed his long repertoire and followed his daydream. There is nothing sexier than an electric guitar, long riffs and a wintry night near the hearth with the man you love.

· · ·

Two years after she bought him the expensive rhinestone-studded guitar case, their relationship soured. One day, while she was at the grocery store, she saw him walking with a black woman. He was carrying the expensive guitar case. She was carrying a plain maroon leather case, very beat up, but it suited her. There was nothing false about this woman: she was raggedy, disheveled in appearance, down to her baggy hip-hop jeans, but she seemed utterly confident in her skin. The two were laughing together, chatting in their own musician's language. There was no evidence that they were lovers and that they were not just friends with music in common. But the fact that he had never mentioned this woman before or that she had never set foot in their house made Mei Ling suspicious. "Knowledge is what corrupts marriages," her grandmother once said. "If you pretend to be an ignorant donkey, you won't know that somebody is riding you." And before she died, she had this to say about Mei Ling's troubled marriage: "Don't tread too lightly. You will forget that you're carrying a burden of cow manure." Oh hell, something got lost in the translation.

He was supposed to be looking for a job, but instead he was hanging around with this black woman, smoking pot, jamming. Mei Ling was not jealous of a possible affair between them, but oddly, she was jealous that this woman had a proprietary dignity about her. She "owned" her art while Mei Ling had always deferred to others first, and as a result, had postponed her novel indefinitely. And what about the choices she had made? Which should be the obvious choice? The ownership of a husband, or the ownership of one's art?

Mei Ling drove around for a couple of hours, fuming. When she finally got home, he was already busy practicing a new composition. He said, "This one is called 'Manifest Destiny.' *Oh, baby, can't you hear the calvary, can't you see the bloody prairie?* I think that I really have a hit this time, baby, really."

"No, I can't hear shit," she said. "It doesn't sound like anything. It sounds like bad guitar playing. I have been listening to you banging that crap for years. Postmodern sampling, punk-jazz fusion, bullshit. I'm tired of your appropriating everybody else's experience while you don't have a single original idea in that teeny brain of yours. Sorry, baby, I've passed the honeymoon stage. You ain't ever gonna revive that stupid garage band of yours. You don't have any vision as an artist. Forget about your rock 'n' roll pipe dreams. You're forty-two—it ain't gonna happen. Jesus was crucified at thirty-three. Buddha obtained enlightenment at thirty-two. You could've 'compromised' and got a teaching job. But no! You couldn't lower yourself to be pedestrian. But deep inside, you knew that your PhD was a crock! The only reason why you wrote your dissertation on *the problems of male whiteness* was because you were trying to be cool and sucked up to your brilliant black professors! You're not a misunderstood genius waiting to be discovered by Dr. Dre and David Geffen. You're a fuckin' middle-aged failure, and I'm tired of paying the bills!"

She couldn't divorce him soon enough and summoned her lawyer to draw up the settlement within six weeks. She had to give him half of the house, which she purchased with her hard-working teacher's salary. But what the hell, it was the price of freedom, for which she paid happily. After all, she had fresh immigrant blood coursing in her veins. She could bounce back and start all over. She could go back to start a new chapter of her long-awaited novel, in which she would make a futuristic turn: the protagonists would be the one-millionth wave of immigrants. In this world, the denizens are not white, brown or black, but purple. They are highly efficient creatures, each equipped with both a vagina and a penis for self-procreation. Their world would not be merely international but intergalactical. All the citizens would carry open passports and move freely through a boundless, borderless existence. There would be no Darwinian, capitalist competition, no wars over land or oil. Finally, humankind would discover contentment. Then, after a long night's rest, she discarded her new ideas completely. "Nah, art is for poseurs and having great ideas is grossly overrated," she decided.

The next night, her dead grandmother came to her in a dream and said, "Don't cry, little mooncake. Work hard, save money, open up a small but tasty restaurant in the neighborhood." And thus, like a good common immigrant girl, she accomplished just what the Great Matriarch apparition predicted. First, she opened Wong's Double Happiness Café in a battered strip mall in Orange County. Almost overnight, it became the darling of southern California. It would be a favorite hangout joint for all the up-and-coming minor starlets.

In the next few years, Mei Ling would open up ten more cafés on the West Coast, then build up a successful franchise system throughout the continent. Ready or not, Wong's Double Happiness Cafés would dot the landscape of America with over three thousand franchises, and our once dreamy, idealistic, failed poet/novelist would become a willy-nilly late capitalist bitch in her middle years and be resigned to living a superficial petty bourgeois life with her adopted spoiled-rotten Russian children, two Cairn Terriers, three Siamese cats . . . happily ever after. Or, not!

Happiness: A Manifesto

The sun shines through the jacaranda trees, the purple flowers opening, opening imperceptibly. And it is only Donny and me, Donny and the feeling of him inside me. And that strong angle of descent, the visage of his fleshy, tanned torso—starting from his sinewy neck, down past his swollen yet hard chest clavicle, down to his groin.

His beauty, his male beauty, is a feeling that I *know*. It is not anything that I could sum up, pontificate on, illuminate via a terse and explosive gender discussion with my radical women friends. On our "mindful" level, in the great dialectic of things, he shall always be the hegemonist/oppressor/invader. The imperialist other—who keeps us oppressed, dissatisfied, yearning. As politically correct as I am, in that verbal bliss of the university, despite my own personal contentment, I continue the usual feminist, dyed-in-the-wool diatribe against male domination: jeer at that Hemingway specialist down the hall with his love of spare, laconic fishing lore—or at Moby Dick reduced to some male patriarchal writer's swollen cock, too large to be conquered in one sitting.

Yet, this woman of the world secretly goes home and lives for a simpler love—somebody to look over the Beaujolais and say,

"Darling, the pasta is superb," that wonderful combination of garlic and extra-extra virgin olive oil, that pungent tang of fresh Roma tomatoes and, of course, the secret three fingers of green chilies preserved in vinaigrette a la Donny. Naked under his rococo apron, he would hum Debussy and meander in our small connubial kitchen, strutting all that love he harbors in his beautiful heart. He is the softer part of my "double consciousness." When I cross his threshold, I could kick off my sensible shoes, slither into my silky, sequined skin, lie back like some self-appointed goddess. And all weekend long, the birds are chirruping and the sea is savagely beautiful. And we would feast and fuck, feast and fuck, breaking all the ideological barriers until Monday morning.

When the cold slap of "conviction" jars me awake and I put on that scruffy, postcolonial tweed jacket and forge onward to the local southern California State University to teach Introduction to American Ethnic Literature, I, the infernal goddess—with hanks of black unruly hair, thick wire-rimmed spectacles, brown sensible shoes—I shall represent all the oppressed female intellectuals of the Third World. I shall begin each day by reminding these spoiled blond surfing children that their forefathers were slave owners, their grandfathers were Chinamen killers, their fathers were patriarchal pigs, their boyfriends were possible rapists, their presidents were institutional criminals, their police force—a testosterone parade with nightsticks and battering rams.

. . .

And this month, in my office I call "the tenth orifice," I shall secretly preside over meetings with five powerful women litigators to initiate Project Alpha. We shall try to find a loophole in the university law code to get rid of fraternities forever—those hellholes that suck up decent, malleable young men and turn them into opportunistic, money-grubbing, women-raping, racist, war-mongering, hegemonic Republicans! We have dubbed our secret society "The Nutcracker Suite." At least two of us are black belts in some exotic martial art form. I, naturally, fancy Wing Chun, a close-range form invented by a very small Chinese woman, four feet tall, eighty-five pounds. The idea is to move closer into the opponent, that is, two inches from his chest, in a deceptive embrace gesture—and then—*poww*—a short fist up the nose. He would see stars and a burst of technicolored rainbows before a panoramic blackness grips him.

Meanwhile, five o'clock chimes like Big Ben on my cell phone. My shoulders shrink back to normal size, and a smile spreads across my face, a pinkness blossoms, and I am hungry and wet and thinking about my love—and how wonderful it would be to have his beautiful penis within me. I want him, this instant, as I am writing my last memo of the day, an endearing note via email to my chairperson.

"Dear Chairperson George Washington Franklin Hancock—your memo of yesterday, regarding reinstating the 'canon' as the mainstay of our literature department, disturbs us greatly. It rings of fascism, reactionary racism and sexism—and we, the *Feminist Nutcracker Suite*, demand that you illuminate us as to your true intentions." (Secretly, I still adore some of the dead male writers like a rich opium I snort privately behind closed doors. Inhaling goopy lines of Keats is an onerous addiction I acquired during graduate school. I get turned on to his poetic death rattle: the sputum coagulating in his frail lungs, his coughing, hacking blood while he woos in that great European epistolary tradition, and ooooh, how a lugubrious love sonnet to Fanny makes me sticky.)

Now back to my paltry email and to that great tradition of email invective . . . and right on the word "intentions"—which I guess the impingement is upon the absent modifiers of "good" or "bad"—and the word "bad" conjures many a wonderful fucking vignette involving Donny and myself.

. . .

One particularly succulent episode was executed in "my tenth orifice" during a sudden California earthquake delivered by the gods. Donny and I had the most glorious October morning defibrillating on my desk. I remember the elaborate maneuvering. First we had to remove my computer and laser printer and place them gracefully on the floor, then unstack and restack my present research on a Cantonese women's colony—silkworm breeders who collectively swore to be celibate and never marry. Although it had not been thoroughly documented, the entire colony of eight-thousand-plus silkworm breeders and mulberry tree attendants were known to be militant lesbians. I visited this village in 2001. To my dismay, the research turned out to be long, personal, boring narratives on horticulture and fish emulsion, peatmoss/ nitrates/human fertilizer/humus and the mandibles of caterpillars! And in the lack of metaphorical interest—there were no fructifying double entendres to be found—I couldn't pry them open to talk about their sex lives. The project bored me and I had long abandoned it—seventy-six audio-recordings/historical agricultural books/copious notes and all—to collect dust on the nethercorner of my giant, power desk!

Now, when Donny and I finally removed this dinosaur off— oh, the dusty spines and femurs—paper clips, note cards, CDs galore—for a morning of naughty, insolent, remarkable romping, and I had stripped away that invaluable red thong with a slit on my woolly aperture, my love slipped comfortably in, his halberd slightly irritating my entry. He was biting my ear, uttering the most salacious dreams in all of the western empire. In "my tenth orifice," we traveled the world. He was the tour guide, whispering in my ear, in Catalan and Ute and various hybrid argots, offering all kinds of delectable treats—half-naked mulatto boys on the beach of Pago Pago, in and out and astride the leaning tower of Pisa, in and out and astride the capsule of Gemini, betwixt and between the sarcophagi of that gilded boy Tut and Chin Shih Huang-ti. Ooooohhhh baby, he murmured, Ohhh Bathsheba, Oohh Lesbia, Oohh Mary Magdalene, Oohh the tundras, the prairies, Oohh the furrows of the Dead Sea. How he plowed me backward and forward until I couldn't remember my race, my color, my destiny—"Gender Studies" now rendered moot or just the name of some dusty journal printed in Indiana. My postcolonial "position" at this moment was "prone." And now, as his finger was focusing on my ninth aperture, his penis was fulfilling my tenth and his tongue was deeply spelunking in my fifth and most cavernous enterprise.

Suddenly, he said something terribly appalling: "I am fucking you now in the bathroom of your grandmother's Hong Kong flat." I finally balked. Now, there are forbidden avenues—fruits that should be left unplucked, frocks to be left unsullied. "Oh, all right, all right, forget that last narrative about the bathroom of your grandmother's Hong Kong flat. How about in the callaloo of your father's giant wok? Yes, that is wonderful. That is a way to get back at him, for abandoning your mother, for making you peel ten thousand shrimps in his restaurant in the summer of 1989." We know it is the end of Confucian world order when filial piety meets the erogenous zone.

Then he whispered, "In the heavens. We are now fucking in the heavens." I said, "I can't. I just happen to be a radical, feminist, Marxist, Chinese American poet who believes in God. *She* would not approve." He continued, rocking me back and forth, in and out. The metal desk under my ass felt cold. The friction of the metal against my thigh against the plaster wall. The cultural anthropologist next door pounded, "Hey, hey, what in hell are you doing? Hanging pictures? Fucking again, Ms. Asian American Poet!" And I let Donny harpoon me as I howled my humpback whale mating call.

. . .

Against our throbbing and pounding and the abstract melody of a busy campus in rain. Against the murmuring of our most *verboten* fantasies. Against the Zen of willful subversion, we fucked. A distant telephone rang in the dark corridor. Nearby, my colleague, Dr. So-and-So Smith, was having a loud confrontation with an enraged Pocahontas. "You gave me a B, you pig," we heard her say. And suddenly, in slow motion, the giant metal shelf cradling the A through Z of major and minor female literary geniuses started toppling: Alcott, Aidoo, Bradstreet, Aphra Behn (sadly unopened), two Brontës as stout bookends, Browning (Liz and not Bob), Bishop (collected) and Mama Gwendolyn Brooks (fraught with Christmas greetings), Cather and Cixous, Chopin (Kate, not the pianist), Dickinson, Doolittle, Eliot (George and not Tom), hooks and Hurston and Hong Kingston, Jordan (O sister river!), Li (not Po but Ch'ing Chao), Lessing (lots of her), Lowell (Amy's embarrassing Chinoiserie . . . well, better than Robert's iambic doldrums), Minh-ha and Mew, McCullers poised with cigarette, the Beloved Toni M. spine to spine with the naughty Anais N., Rhys, Rossetti, Rich (lots of her), Gerty, Gerty, Gayatri, down to Stein and Sojourner—Truth is truth is truth, Silko and Mary Shelley rolled off the shelves like tongues of the twisted sea, down past Wheatley, Wordsworth (a small pamphlet of Dorothy's), down to Untermeyer (ughh, how did that mangy anthology get there?), down to yet another misplaced but resurrected male poet named Zukofsky (got that for Christmas from some pedantic L=A=N=G=U=A=G=E poet). The shelves came tumbling down. O Mother Jericho, what a historical occasion! How appropriately synchronized with our orgasmic paroxysms! The walls waved. The earth grimaced a giant gaping chasm. We stayed attached, cock and cunt, two multi-limbed creatures, fucking for dear life!

Three Endings

Mei Ling is walking home from school and is confronted by three bullies. Each of them has a mean dog by his side. One, a tall blond boy, is with a Doberman pinscher and is walking toward her from the north. The second, a stocky brown boy with a big pit bull, is walking toward her from the east. The last, a short boy, naturally, has a little yappy Chihuahua running after him like a girly-girl. They all hate Mei Ling for no reason at all, as you can tell. Perhaps they hate Chinese people. Perhaps they hate her because she gets straight As. Perhaps it was because one of them called her "wetback-gook," and she yelled back "trailer-trash loser." Perhaps she said, "Your Mama." Perhaps she flipped them twin birds from a hilltop and stuck her tongue out at them. Perhaps it wasn't she who perpetuated these things, but her nasty twin, Moonie. And because the boys are afraid of Moonie's mean fists, they're getting back at Mei Ling instead. She doesn't know why they hate her, but they do!

So she runs south as fast as her little legs can manage. And she runs and runs. Finally, she stops at a ritzy five-story apartment building and climbs up a lattice of plush green ivy which reaches all the way up to the rooftop. Halfway up, she realizes that the lattice is broken and now she is climbing only ivy. Her little hands and feet are sustained only by the raw knots of the vines. The boy with the Doberman and the boy with the pit bull are closing in on either side.

Having ridden the elevator up, the boy and the Chihuahua are already on the roof. They are looking down at her now. The Chihuahua, with a little white and black coat, is now gnawing on the vine. Mei Ling is hanging on a taut piece of vine near a fourth-story window. She will plunge to the ground any minute now. The two boys and the big dogs are at the bottom, waiting for her to fall, to tear her into pieces.

ENDING NO. 1

Mei Ling reaches to her backpack and into a secret compartment. With her right arm gripping the vine, she pulls out a mini-mooncake with her left. It is from the last batch her grandmother made before she died. First, she nibbles around the outside brown crust until it's all gone, then she stuffs the entire naked cakie into her mouth. She sucks on the gooey lotus paste to get to the yummy egg yolk. She looks over her shoulder—the sky is pale blue and translucent. She is calm and contented, and her heart holds no regrets. Nothing more wonderful than the sweetness of this moment. How sweet, how sweet it is.

ENDING NO. 2

Mei Ling reaches to her backpack and into the secret compartment. She pulls out three mini-mooncakes. She throws one up to the Chihuahua on the rooftop. The Chihuahua catches it in one leap and loves the sticky sweetness, then barks and wags its tail for more. She throws two down to the boys. They both catch them and stuff them into their mouths. She shouts, "Hey, I also have pork buns for the big dogs, and soft red and purple licorice sticks from Zack's." Her grandmother had always said, "Sweeten your mouth, sweeten your words, and all will be peaceful under heaven." Mei Ling climbs down the ivy. They all sit down under a giant coral tree and share Mei Ling's sweet goodies. Finally, after months of fighting, they resolve their differences.

ENDING NO. 3

Mei Ling reaches to her backpack and pulls out two mini-mooncakes. They are really deathstars dipped in blowfish poison and disguised as mooncakes. They are the last secret weapons that her grandmother gave her before she died. Her grandmother said to keep them with her always, but use them only in the most dire of situations. She throws one at the Doberman, hits him between the eyes, and he falls. The poison makes him convulse on the ground. She throws another at the pit bull and pierces his ribcage. He spins around and around frothing in the mouth. The boy on the rooftop grabs his yapping Chihuahua and runs into the building. The other two boys leave their dying dogs and run for their lives. One shouts, "I'll kill you tomorrow at nine, you slant-eyed bitch."

Mei Ling climbs up to the rooftop and discovers that some rich white lady had built a paradise roof-garden (actually, it wasn't she who built it, but her arbor guy, Jesús, who planted the trees and her gardener, Truong, who seeded the veggies and flowers).

There are terra-cotta pots of palmettos and dwarf maples all around. Bright red tomatoes and ripened strawberries fill giant wooden planters. All the excitement has sent chills to Mei Ling's bladder, so she pulls down her jeans and pees into the tomatoes. Then she stuffs five of the fattest strawberries into her pockets and one into her mouth, sweetening all the way home.

Postscript/Some Notes

As much as I loved creating these wild tales about the raucous twins Moonie and Mei Ling and their dominating grandmother, I equally enjoyed excavating hundreds of Chinese and other Asian tales in my continuous research and preparation. I spent years staying up to wee hours reading Chinese ghost stories, "records of the strange," historical treatises, the ancient philosophical texts of Zhuangzi, Laozi and Confucius, popular kung fu revenge tales, manga comic books, minority-Chinese folktales and animal fables, as well as reams of radical Zen texts and Buddhist scripture that date back to the Pala era. Sometimes I suffered through terrible translations; sometimes I bolstered my reading with several cumbersome dictionaries so that I could better delve into the riches of the original text.

I remember my own grandmother as a major transmitter of apocryphal family lore that was imbedded with useful moral lessons, aimed at keeping the girlchild selfless and obedient. I especially remember one tale about a virtuous Chin niece, three branches removed on my grandfather's side, who rejected several fine suitors, stayed unmarried, held four jobs and took care of her sick mother and twelve wounded siblings until she dropped dead suddenly at the age of forty-three. She was so virtuous that even in death she could not relinquish her responsibilities. It was reported that her ghost lingered around the village for decades, forever vigilant over her people, humming old songs and picking flowers.

It must be a profound disappointment to grandmothers everywhere that ultimately the imagination loves chaos and rebellion more than it loves reverence. For every reverent tale about an obedient, filial girl who sacrifices all for her family, there are ten about demon fox-girls who sexually ravage lonely scholars in the middle of the night, sometimes tearing them apart from limb to limb. Not to mention crazy monks who feel the need to shatter all preconceived notions of conventional Buddhism for the sake of quick enlightenment . . . for it must be the irreverent, rebellious inner child in them who dares to mumble a shocking koan such as, "To know the Buddha one must kill the Buddha," and then compares "the world honored one" to a bag of flax and a shit stick.

. . .

The following are random notes that might help the reader unravel various allusions and primary sources that inspired many of the tales in this book.

p. 30 Fish are happy: This phrase alludes to the following vivid conversation in my favorite Daoist tale, a classic by Zhuangzi (fourth century):

> One day Zhuangzi and Huizi are strolling leisurely on a bridge.
> Zhuangzi says: "Look at the happy fish, darting about in the river."
> Huizi says: "How do you know that fish are happy? You are not a fish."
> Zhuangzi says: "You are not I. How do you know that I don't know that fish are happy?"

p. 48 Ax Handle: This title alludes to a ballad in the great Confucian classic "Book of Songs":

> In hewing an ax-handle
> The pattern is not far off

Meaning: one must grip the ax handle, which is the model for an ax handle itself, to make another ax handle; a philosophical remark about influence and the continuity of art.

p. 86 Awkward Homi Bhabha sentence: The passage written by Homi Bhabha is from Emily Eakin, "Harvard's Prize Catch, a Delphic Postcolumnist," *New York Times*, November 17, 2001. See also Homi K. Bhabha, ed., *Nation and Narration*, New York, Routledge, 1990.

p. 107 Thirteen Buddhist Tales: Many of these pieces are parodies of famous Buddhist and Zen tales and koans, but filtered through the contemporary context of Moonie and Mei Ling's lives.

p. 111 That Ancient Parable: This alludes to two famous Zen stories by Master Nanzen or Nan Chuan (748–839), and Master Gutei Isshi or Jùzhī Yīzhǐ (dates unknown, tale dates back to ninth century). These two tales are very disturbing due to their violence and work against the Buddhist principles of being compassionate toward all creatures and not causing injury to sentient beings. Such tales are meant to be shocking to awaken the pupil from conventional thinking and force them to quick enlightenment.

Nanzen's Cat:

Two monks were fighting over a cat. Nanzen picked up the cat in front of all the disciples and said, "If one of you can say the correct word, the cat will be saved, if not I will kill it." Nobody could offer an answer. Thereupon, Nanzen killed the cat.

Gutei's Finger:

Whenever someone asked Master Gutei about Zen, he would raise his forefinger into the air. A boy in the village walked around and imitated this very gesture. One day, the Master Gutei stopped the boy and cut off his finger with a knife. The boy ran off, crying in pain . . . but when the Master called to him, the boy stopped his crying and turned to look. Gutei raised his finger into the air. The boy attained instant enlightenment.

p. 112 Putai, or the Happy Buddha: Putai is depicted in scrolls and sculpture to be fat, laughing and often surrounded by children. He is a very popular icon and appears on Chinese mothers' mantels all over the diaspora. He represents prosperity and fertility, which is contradictory to the Buddhist idea of detachment and austere simple living.

p. 114 Ryokan's Moon: Taigu Ryokan (1758–1831), nickname: Great Fool. "Ryokan's Moon" alludes to a story about the impoverished monk Ryokan who walked into his hut and caught a thief ransacking his drawers. He took off his ragged clothing and gave them to the thief, and said, "Sorry, you have found nothing here to steal, please take my clothes." Then, he stared at the moon and said, " I wish I could have given him the moon."

p. 116 The Equanimity of All Things: From Zhuangzi's "Discussion on Making Things Equal":

> *When the monkey trainer handed out chestnuts, he said to the monkeys, "I give you three in the morning and four in the afternoon." The monkeys were furious at this news. So the trainer revised his proposition and said, "I'll give you four in the morning and three in the afternoon." Thus, the monkeys were satisfied.*

p. 117 Sajani: In Nepal, every few years a young girl is selected to become a "Kumari," a "Living Goddess," and will hold her reign until she menstruates. She is supposed to be a perfect, unblemished beauty and come from the Shakya caste, the caste to which Buddha belonged. Sajani began her reign in 2007, but controversy arose because she traveled to the United States to promote a documentary film in which she appeared. She was forced to retire in 2008.

p. 120 Wiping One's Ass with the Sutras: This story alludes to a Sung Dynasty koan:

> *A young monk asked Ummon, " What is the Buddha?"*
> *Ummon answers, "A dried shit stick."*

The Chinese used bamboo sticks for toilet paper.

p. 121 The Theory of the One Hand: For centuries Zen learning has been transmitted from master to disciple in the form of absurd riddles and intense question-and-answer sessions called koans (Japanese: *kōan*; Chinese: *gōng-àn*). They are designed to be nonsensical, circuitous, often shocking and humorous to force the student to relinquish conventional thinking and thereby achieve instant enlightenment.

The famous koan "Two hands clap and there is a sound; what is the sound of one hand?" is attributed to Hakuin (1686–1769), who revived the koan tradition in Japan.

p. 124 Lantau: This is an island outside of Hong Kong, on which sits the largest bronze Buddha in the world. It measures 110 feet tall and weighs 280 tons.

p. 125 Beasts of Burden: In Buddhist thought, animals are considered sentient beings, lesser in intellectual ability but capable of feeling suffering. They possess "Buddha" nature and have the potential of being enlightened. Buddha was compassionate toward all creatures and preached his first sermon in Deer Park, among the animals.

However, in the reincarnation hierarchy, to be reborn as an animal is considered "low" rebirth. The animal realm is treacherous, and animals live in constant fear of being attacked and eaten by others or are forced to hard labor and to eventual slaughter.

Throughout the book, I tried to keep Buddha's compassionate presence in my animal characters, especially in this part called "Beasts of Burden." The pieces are allegorical fables, revitalized in the postcolonial and contemporary American context.

The epigraph refers to one of the many trials of the quail, which was purported to be one of the animal souls that Buddha inhabited in his past lives.

p. 132 Fox Girl: Throughout Chinese literary history, hundreds of stories about fox demons are transmitted orally from generation to generation as well as anthologized in numerous historical volumes of ghost stories in the "Zhiguai" tradition.

While researching through texts in the Harvard-Yenching Library, I read about a fox demon who turned herself into a beautiful girl and appeared in front of a poor scholar for midnight copulation. In some versions, she stays for one night; in others, she stays for years, has children with the scholar, murders him, then disappears into ether. I am updating this tale, with Mei Ling turning into a fox and then copulating with a famous poet. It is a satire about the academic poetry scene.

p. 139 Cicada: For two years, I carried this beautiful fragment from the Diamond Sutra in my purse:

> *The egg-born, the womb-born, the moisture-born, those with form, those without form, those with consciousness, those without consciousness, those who are neither conscious nor unconscious . . .*

p. 202 Three Endings: This refers to a famous Sung Dynasty Zen strawberry tale:

> *A man encountered a tiger in an open field. The tiger chased him over a cliff. The man grabbed on to a strong vine growing on the side of the cliff and held on with dear life. Above him the tiger paced and growled. Below him, another hungry tiger waited for him to fall. And to make things worse, two mice, one black, one white, were gnawing on the vine. He would plunge to his death any moment now. He saw some strawberries growing within reach. He held fast to the vine with one hand and plucked a ripe strawberry with the other. It was sweet, very sweet.*

Some scholars dispute the ending of this story and accuse the early English translators of corrupting the ending to please a Western audience. A strawberry is a cultivated western fruit and can't possibly appear wild and on a cliff in Sung Dynasty China. A more accurate translation of the plant would be Chinese "bayberry." In some of the Chinese and Japanese versions, the berry is poisonous. Therefore, the ending in the original version may be much bleaker than that of the famous tale in translation.

Acknowledgments

I would like to thank the United States Artists Foundation, the Radcliffe Institute for Advanced Study at Harvard, the Lannan Foundation, the Rockefeller Foundation Bellagio Center, the Corporation of Yaddo, Headlands Center for the Arts, the Stadler Poetry Center at Bucknell University and San Diego State University. I thank Bob Grunst, who faithfully served as my first reader for many of these tales. I thank Severino Reyes for his keen proofreading eye. I thank Ken Weisner, Miriam Kuznets and Sandra Zane for serving as emergency outside readers. I thank Don Lonewolf for his undying love. I thank my editor, Jill Bialosky, and my agent, Sandy Djkstra, for their continuous support. I thank Adrienne Davich and the posse at Norton. I am grateful to the editors of the publications in which these stories (or earlier versions) first appeared:

Paris Review: "Lantau"
Harvard Review: "After Enlightenment, There Is Yam Gruel"
Feminist Studies: "Fox Girl"
Prairie Schooner: "Beast of Burden," "Ax Handle," "The Wolf and the Chinese Pug" (winners of the Glenna Luschesi Award)
Indiana Review: "Parable of the Cake," "Parable of the Fish"
Zzyva: "Liars," "Happiness: A Manifesto"
Michigan Quarterly Review: "Round Eyes," "Singing Worm"
Crate: "Duets"
Seattle Review: "Parable of Squab"

ANTHOLOGIES

Charlie Chan Is Dead, edited by Jessica Hagedorn, Penguin, New York: 1994: "Moon"

Charlie Chan Is Dead 2: At Home in the World, edited by Jessica Hagedorn, Penguin, New York, 2003: "Moon," "Parable of the Cake"

InvAsians, edited by Evelyn Rodriguez, Asian Women United, Berkeley, CA, 2004: "Round Eyes"

On a Bed of Rice: An Asian American Erotic Feast, edited by Geraldine Kudaka, Doubleday, New York, 1995: "Happiness: A Manifesto"

The Pushcart Prize, Pushcart Press, Yonkers, NY, 1995: "Happiness: A Manifesto"

Bear Flag Republic, edited by Gary Young and Christopher Buckley, Greenhouse Review Editions, Santa Cruz, CA, 2008: "Why Men Are Dogs," "That Ancient Parable about Nanzen's Doll/Gutei's Finger, Redux," "Impermanence"

Hunger and Thirst, edited by Nancy Cary, City Works Press, 2008: "After Enlightenment, There Is Yam Gruel"

He just wanted a decent book to read ...

Not too much to ask, is it? It was in 1935 when Allen Lane, Managing Director of Bodley Head Publishers, stood on a platform at Exeter railway station looking for something good to read on his journey back to London. His choice was limited to popular magazines and poor-quality paperbacks – the same choice faced every day by the vast majority of readers, few of whom could afford hardbacks. Lane's disappointment and subsequent anger at the range of books generally available led him to found a company – and change the world.

'We believed in the existence in this country of a vast reading public for intelligent books at a low price, and staked everything on it'
Sir Allen Lane, 1902–1970, founder of Penguin Books

The quality paperback had arrived – and not just in bookshops. Lane was adamant that his Penguins should appear in chain stores and tobacconists, and should cost no more than a packet of cigarettes.

Reading habits (and cigarette prices) have changed since 1935, but Penguin still believes in publishing the best books for everybody to enjoy. We still believe that good design costs no more than bad design, and we still believe that quality books published passionately and responsibly make the world a better place.

So wherever you see the little bird – whether it's on a piece of prize-winning literary fiction or a celebrity autobiography, political tour de force or historical masterpiece, a serial-killer thriller, reference book, world classic or a piece of pure escapism – you can bet that it represents the very best that the genre has to offer.

Whatever you like to read – trust Penguin.